Christina Bunk
Christiane Geissler
Ole Frahm
João Guimarães
Olga Bosch
Stefanie Hetze
Marius Kob
Benjamin Renter
Ronny Willisch
Gunta Lauck
Björn Liebchen
Frieder Butzmann
Gamma Bak
Carita Najewitz
Henriette Huppmann
Klaus Dieter Ryrko
Jörn Eickholt
Michael Brynntrup
Bazon Brock
Lydia Nsiah
Emily Young
Gerd Roscher
Dominik Schleier
Tom van Vliet
Sandra Gabbert
Erik Pawassar
Anne-Lena Boettcher
Gabriele Sparwasser
Lars Rudolph
Familie Pues
Marion Götz
Anja Finkous
Ellen Lippok
János Kepes
Maren Hobein
Péter Krausz
Ulrich Hagel
Claudia Loest
Oliver Elias
Simone Lütgert
Ulrike Bauer
Alexander Strathern
Jörg Weidauer

Georg Marioth
Jagna Lewandowska
Gerhard Schumm
Micha Redeligx
Eray Egilmez
Anna Anders
Christoph Römer
Dore Sooth
Matthias Neumann
Christine Kummer
Beate Blasius
Michaela Ott
Peter Weibel
Udita Egelhof
Rosemarie Knaur
Margot Mählmann
Gisela Schulz
Markus Stein
Carl-Ludwig Rettinger
Hermann Reimer
Ulrike Schimming
Florian Zeyfang
Katrin Küchler
Ebba Jahn
László Révész
Sylke Gottlebe
Hartmut Bomhoff
Nathalie David
Susanne Kreutzer
Christian Schmitz
Gabriele Boulanger
Moritz Peters
Ina Schröder
Klaus Lüttmer
Friederike Greul
Sabine Dingel
Marc Fleischer-Pratschke
Ludger Derenthal
Inga Knelke
Reinhard Bestgen
Ralf Simon
Penelope Wehrli
Oliver Geisler

Julia Tervoort
Martin Tervoort
Thomas Tode
Jeanpaul Goergen
Pia Riedel
Wolfram Riedel
Brigitte Barcklow
Petra Junold
Judit Kepes
Serafina Morrin
E. Brinkmann to Broxten
Kathrin Becker
Atau Hámos
Isidor Hámos
Ariella Hirshfeld
Hennink Stöve
Timothy Schulz
Dagmar Dreßler
Claudia Schwarte
Conny E. Voester
Maki Satake
Keitaro Oshima
Jasmine Ghandtchi
Karl Winter
Thomas Kutschker
David Blair
Tim Kellner
Henriette Sachse
Manuel Feifel
Annette Heinisch
Mirjam Wenzel
Nathilde Overrein Rapp
Chistoph Dreher
Till Egelhof
Anja Pratschke
Heike Salchli
Anka Schmid
Joachim Wittern
Ulrike Mattern
Joel Bennett
Patty Walker
Nicole von Blume
Patrick von Blume

Matl Findel
Flora Hirshfeld
Gerd Mittelberg
Isabelle Redfern
Karolina Ferencz
Reto Ott
Florian Illies
Christian Mahler
Finbarr Morrin
Christoph Steyer
Maria Winkler
Gerhard Moser
Kai Riedel
Pieter Egelhof
Stephan Kühne
Pascal Cling
Wanda Pratschke
Ruth Bierich
H. Quinque-Wessel
Sybille Badstübner
András Forgách
Walter Schmitt-Jamin
Stefan Gerhard
Péter Forgács
Marcel Marburger
Dietrich Leder
Silke Grossmann

*Many thanks to
all supporters!*

FIASCO

A photonovel by Janet Riedel,
Katja Pratschke and Gusztáv Hámos

With fragments from Imre Kertész' book

Time travel images
An introduction by GUSZTÁV HÁMOS

Imre Kertész' novel *Fiasco* is permeated with the phenomenon of the Kafkaesque: you return home to what is an apparently alien city. Already on the first morning, you are awoken by the postman delivering your notice of dismissal and that you are now "broke." Kertész' protagonist Köves[1] is not only penniless, but has also been robbed of his space and time: he has been "allocated" a room as a lodger and is also not allowed to avail of his time on his own: "He had been handed his papers for the job at the steelworks and told to present them at the press department of the Ministry for Production, and without delay moreover, lest the greater part of the remainder of the working day be lost, and in order that Köves might be set immediately to work at the Ministry, should they see fit. Köves had rushed from one tram to another—the Ministry was near the city centre, a long way from the factory—as if he had been handed some extraordinarily fragile public property: his time, which he had to deliver perfectly intact to its destination, taking care, above all, not even to dream of pilfering any part of it for himself." (pp. 246, 247)[2] Thus, Köves does not have any time. And not because of his numerous activities, for instance, but because the time he needs to develop his capabilities to achieve his self-fulfillment does not belong to him. That which is preventing Köves from availing of his life's time can neither be surmounted nor circumvented. Köves is suffering from time dis-possess-ion. Consequently, he experiences time as interminable and nothing at one and the same time: "Ever since arriving in the country, Köves had always had a spot of trouble with time; while living it, it seemed interminable to him, but when he thought about it as the past, it seemed practically nothing, with a duration that might have fitted into a single hour [...] and ultimately, it fleetingly occurred to Köves, an entire lifetime was going to pass like that, his life, on which he would eventually be able to look back with the thought that he could have seen to it within the space of a single hour, the rest being a sheer frittering away of time, difficult living conditions, struggle—and all for what?" (pp. 247, 248)

The conclusion may thus be drawn that the perception of time is dependent on the fate, the destiny, of each person. And whoever has a fate also has the time required for it. But, by contrast, one who is "fateless" cannot avail of their time, not to develop their capabilities and also not in the form of their destiny.

When Köves needs time for "private matters," he has to steal it, to attain it through

---

1 Köves is Hungarian for stone.
2 Imre Kertész: *Fiasco*, New York, Melville House Publishing, 2001. All of the page numbers in brackets refer to the novel *Fiasco*.

thievery, to become a "day thief." In the world in which Köves has "landed," day thievery or parasitism is regarded, as Kertész writes in one of the South Seas parts of *Fiasco*, as damage to the "common good." And there is a legal punishment provided for that, namely deportation to a labor camp. (The reintroduction of this form of punishment has been discussed by the rightwing populist government in Hungary since 2012.) The fateless Köves knows labor camps from an earlier time in his life, and he knows very well that work does not bring freedom there.[3] Work time was never a time of freedom, but rather a degrading enforcement. The people were abused in the camps as slaves, and murdered in the end.

Death is—according to Bazin—the "victory of time." The victory of time is an absurdity as such, a paradox: when a human dies, they cease to age, and thus through their death they conquer time. The price for this is life itself, which is absolutely necessary in order to be able to consciously perceive time.

"Oh well, time," as Henry Bergson would say: "What an imperfect term (for) between space and duration."

Yet, it is time itself that is difficult to define and to comprehend. But what we are able to comprehend, for that, are the images of light in the photo apparatus or film camera, images determined by and conditional on time.

With the invention of photography, the re-presentation of light reflected on bodies and objects, we suddenly have irrefutable proof right here of something that has been. With the invention of film, the re-presentation of movement from reality in successive phases of image sequences, we turn that which has been into a progressive becoming before our eyes. Photographic sequences, series and successions also form the visual groundwork in the photonovel *Fiasco*, created for the film FIASCO—FRAGMENTS BASED ON THE NOVEL BY IMRE KERTÉSZ (G 2010), which consists solely of photographs. Films that fundamentally consist of still images are what we call photofilms.[4] But when we place a photo in a cinematographic context, or when we look at a photofilm, at that very moment we travel through time. In the context of the fleeting images in film, the photo stands for constancy, even though we are not able to hold it in our hands. The photo in film assures us that what we are seeing now has been there beyond doubt. It gives us this reference to the past in the "cinema's own present" and

---

[3] Wordplay on "Arbeit macht frei"—the cynical sign over the nazi concentration camps.
[4] Gusztáv Hámos, Katja Pratschke, Thomas Tode (ed.), *Viva Fotofilm bewegt/unbewegt/Viva Photofilm Moving/Non-moving*, Marburg, Schüren, 2010.

thus permits us to think (about) all further time dimensions.

The most famous photofilm of all is, beyond doubt, Chris Marker's key work LA JETÉE from 1962. This bleak science-fiction classic about travelling through time begins with a photographic copying process, a kind of double exposure that limits the double presence of the nameless hero — in a déjà-vu — within two time levels: the protagonist finds himself in one place, yet "twice" at the same moment: once as a child and, at the same time, as a grown man. The runway at Orly, to which the hero returns at the end of the film, is the place where he sees himself dying with his own eyes. In this way, the photo is also given a thematic context in the film: the death of the man is placed to an equal extent both in the past (the photo) and in the future (in the progressive becoming of the film).

"With the photonovel *Fiasco*, an homage to LA JETÉE is proposed: in a nameless airport in a large, foreign yet familiar city, a man is searching for a way to survive, in a system which has condemned all those people who have not yet lost their belief in the individual and in freedom."[5]

Unlike the doubly present hero in LA JETÉE, Kertész' protagonist Köves seems to be doubly absent, because he dreams himself into a person alien to him, one whom he does not know and whom he also has nothing to do with: "In short, he loafed around as a displaced person in his own anonymous life [...]." (p. 126) This means that Köves bears a name that is not congruent with his life, and he has a homeland that does not coincide with the place he calls home. The city that Kertész describes is also not congruent temporarily and spatially. After returning from "abroad" (from Auschwitz, from Buchenwald), Köves walks along streets that seem as strange as they are familiar to him. Memories from the city of his birth: Budapest, déjà-vus ("from his dreams, from movies, from travel brochures, from illustrated guidebooks" (p. 141)) overlap with the city he is returning to, and that has evidently changed radically because of the war. Thus, the pairs of images in the photonovel *Fiasco* are also not necessarily congruent with each other. It is far more the case that they attest to temporal-spatial shifts; they are the logical equivalence of conveying the shifts and reflections applied in the novel.

Köves's visions of doubling presumably come from the temporal-spatial oppression he experienced in the concentration camps: when the body finds itself in extreme spatial,

---

5 Nathalie Hénon and Jean-Francois Rettig: *Moving Images, un abécédaire contemporain*, K come Kant, event announcement: Gaîté Lyrique, 9.10.2013.

physical and biological distress, the spirit has to liberate itself from the body, separate from it, in order to be able to survive. As long as the spirit senses desire, the body can survive (somehow), regardless of how withered, maimed and mutilated it may be. The method whereby one removes oneself from physical reality is omnipresent for Köves, because he is exhausted by life and constantly sinking into a deep sleep.

The photonovel did not attempt to illustrate Kertész' book or describe it in images. Instead, it heads off like a detective on a case, tracking down and locating the traces of the "crime" many years after the events in the novel had occurred.

While the photographs to Kertész' book are created in the present, the traces of the bygone social systems reveal themselves clearly in overlappings, in ambivalent concurrences, and in strange doublings. The photographs are marked by ambivalence and ambiguity, shaped by the historic changes. This doubling works like a recollection of the present: with experience and memory separating from each other in the present. During the editing of the texts and images, an overlapping of times is created, a tense ambiguity.

It is not unusual with a book that the images in it are still. When it has movie images in it, we move them reflexively in our thoughts. We think the movement in a manner similar to how we think the movement of the still images in the photofilms as they appear before our eyes in the cinema.

The book with filmic images moves the "reader" to think movement; by flicking through the book, the editing, the montage, is effected through our own exploration. By moving back and forth, the reader can observe the cinematographic book forwards and backwards and determine the time durations in it for themselves.

Arrival Köves came to with a buzzing in his ears; he had probably fallen asleep, almost missing that extraordinary moment when they descended from starlit altitude into earthly night. Scattered flickers of light showed on the borders of a horizon which tilted constantly with the turns of the aircraft. For all he knew, he could be watching a bobbing convoy of ships on the dark ocean. Yet below them was dry land; could the city really present such a pitiable sight? Köves's home came to mind, the other city—Budapest—that he had left. Even though he had already been flying for sixteen hours, it now caught up with him for the first time, like a slight tipsiness, the certainty of the distance which seperated him from the familiar bend of the Danube, the lamp-garlanded bridges, the Buda hills, and the illuminated wreath of the inner city. Here, too, he had glimpsed a faintly glistening band down there, more than likely a river, and above it the odd sparsely lighted arch—those were presumably bridges; and during the descent he had also been able to make out that on one side of the river the city sprawled out over a plain, while on the other side it was set on hillocky terrain.

Köves had no chance to make any further observations. The plane touched down […].

All of the following text fragments are from Imre Kertész, *Fiasco*. New York: Melville House Publishing; Translation © 2011, Tim Wilkinson from *A kudarc*, (2nd edition) Századvég Kiadó, Budapest, 1994.
Albert Camus' essay *The Myth of Sisyphus* is of central importance for Kertész' novel *Fiasco*. The names of the protagonists Köves, Sziklai and Berg translated into English are Stone, Rock and Mountain from this story.

Certain preliminaries He stepped into an empty, lighted hall; only now did Köves see how deceptive the evening had been outside, for here inside he did not find the lighting anything like as bright; to the contrary, it struck him more as gloomy, even gap-toothed here and there, and all in all fairly dingy. The hall itself was large, but in comparison with the arrivals halls of international airports—as witness the deserted desks, empty cashiers' windows, and all the other installations over which he cast but a cursory glance—it was provincially small-scale.

He was assailed by a sensation—absurd, of course—that he had passed that way once before, a sensation caused, perhaps, by all the fake natural stone—on the walls, the floors, every conceivable place—and the distinctive lines of the counters and other furnishings: the mark of a certain taste, one might almost say style, which in mid-century could still be considered modern, but which so easily became outmoded with the passage of fifteen or twenty years. Only this, and then the feeling of exhaustion which was again getting the better of him, could have produced the strange illusion that what he was seeing he had already seen once before, and what was happening had already happened to him once before.

For all that, he didn't know what was going to happen; Köves was suddenly gripped by a lightheaded, submissive, almost liberated feeling of being ready, all at once, to accept any adventure — come what may, whatever might snatch him, carry him off, and engulf him, whereby his life would take a new turn: Wasn't that why he had set off on this journey, after all? Köves's life over there — somewhere into the night, or even beyond that, in the remoteness of limitless tracts, maybe in another dimension, who knows? — had, there was no denying it, hit rock bottom.

It may have begun at birth—or no, rather with his death, or to be more accurate, his rebirth. For Köves had survived his own death; at a certain moment in time when he ought to have died, he did not die, although everything had been made ready for that, it was an organized, socially approved, done deal, but Köves had simply been unwilling to satisfy the circumstances, was unable to withstand the natural instinct for life which was working inside him, not to speak of the good luck on offer, so therefore—defying all rationality—he had stayed alive. Because of that he had been subsequently dogged constantly by a painful sense of provisionality, like someone who is only waiting in a temporary hiding place to be called to account for his negligence [...].

On 19 March 1944, the Germans occupied Hungary. In the Birkenau concentration camp, the expansion of the crematoriums began and a new train line was laid to transport the deportees from Hungary. Imre Kertész was fourteen years old when he was arrested in Budapest and transported to Auschwitz in July 1944. He was subsequently moved to the Zeitz labour camp and then to Buchenwald. After the end of the war and the liberation of the concentration camps, he returned to Budapest in 1945.

In short, he loafed around as a displaced person in his own anonymous life [...].

There was no getting away from it, he had written a novel, but only in the sense that he would have flung himself out of even an aircraft into nothingness in the event of a terminal disaster, if he saw that as the sole possibility for survival; all at once it became obvious to Köves that, figuratively speaking, he could now only hit the ground as a writer or vanish into nothingness.

On waking the next day. Preliminaries. Köves sits down.

Although he had been allocated his home, Köves did not spend the remaining hours of that night in his bed; as to exactly where he did spend them, in the first moments of starting up from an, in all likelihood, brief and light, yet nonetheless all-obliterating dream, maybe he did not know either. The sky had assumed a glassy brightness; his limbs felt stiff and numb, his shoulder blades were pressed up against the back of a bench in the park area of a public square, his neck felt as if it had been dislocated: it could be that as he was sleeping he had simply laid it on the shoulder of the stranger seated next to him, a basically well-built, tubby man wearing a polka-dot bow-tie.

Köves looked disorientedly around: the sparsely placed street lamps were still lit—green-flamed gas lamps on cast-iron posts with spiral ornaments, as in Köves's happier childhood days—and electric lights were glowing here and there in the windows of the grey, shabby houses surrounding the square. Köves could practically hear the bustling going on behind them, the rushed and hasty noises of waking up and getting ready, and was almost waiting for the as yet closed front doors to spring open and people to pour out of the damp doorways and line up in order to be counted. He must have dreamed something, his irrational ideas were mostly likely still being fed by that, yet Köves was netherertheless seized by a disagreeable emotion, a sense of having omitted to do something: he had already been put on a roll call somewhere, he was missing from somewhere, and an irreparable silence would be the response to the strident announcement of his name.

[…] Köves set off on foot with the peculiar assurance of a person led by memory; or by his travel experiences, although he could not boast of any travel experience, nor could memory have guided him in a place he had never been before.

At street corners he was always gripped by the same shy hope: each time he hoped he had lost his way. Yet each and every time he came upon precisely the place he had known in advance, and at worst he did not recognize it immediatly; for instance, in the place of a tall building he might now find a ruin or an empty lot; in place of a specific stretch of street that he would look for in vain, he would find one of a different character yet, in the end, exactly the same.
In Köves's memory, these minutes remained the most testing: he was going around a foreign city with whose every nook and cranny he was nevertheless familiar—a strange sensation […].

The sense of wonder had quit him, bit by bit, he was seized by a benevolent weakness, and in the way he ran his hand over a scabby house wall or a boarded-up shop window, in the way his steps found their way in the already familiar streets, Köves was possessed by that unfamiliar, and yet at the same time relaxed, almost intimate sense of homelessness that was on the verge of suggesting, to an intellect sinking back into dull exhaustion, that he was, indeed, back home.

Dwelling In the entrance hall he was greeted with a musty smell. Only a few of the imitation marble slabs that had faced the walls in the stairwell had remained in place, the elevator did not work, and there were gaps and cracks in the staircase as if iron-toothed beasts were taking bites out of the steps by night. Since he could hear sounds behind his front door: movement, a rapid patter of short steps, a shrill female voice as well as a second, croaking one of more uncertain origin, Köves did not even attempt to use his key—that too he found in the envelope he had been given by the chief customs man—but rather rang the bell so as not to embarrass anyone.

[…] By the sober light of day, naturally, he could not have seriously supposed that he had been accorded the priceless gift of a home of his own; as it was, they had probably done more for him than they had thought—most likely nothing more than a provision that was driven by the pressure of necessity, so they would not have to immediately start shifting him from place to place as a homeless person.

On his return in 1945, Imre Kertész first lived with his mother in Zivatar utca. After completing school, he rented a room as a subtenant in Lógodi utca. Photos: Apartment in Atttila út from the 1950s unchanged since then.

Köves's room opened onto the other side of the hallway, diagonally opposite the kitchen: it was not particularly large, but it was enough for sleeping in and even gave a bit of room to swing a cat, the sort of place, Köves recalled, that back in his childhood had been called "the servant's quarters." It had obviously been designed to be darker, but since the firewall that would normally have overlooked the window—the whole of the next-door house was simply missing, its former site being marked by a dusty pile of rubble on the ground down below—the room was flooded with light [...]. The couch promised to be a good place to lie on—Köves was almost dying to try it out straight away [...].

Köves now started to sink, and he was dreaming before he had even fallen asleep. What he dreamed was that he had strayed into the strange life of a foreigner who was unknown to him and had nothing to do with him, yet still being aware that this was only his dream playing with him, since he was the dreamer and could only dream about his own life.

Dismissal Köves awoke to a sound of ringing, or to be more specific, to having to open the door: it seemed that the impatient ringing, which kept on repeating, at times for protracted periods, at times in fitful bursts, must have pulled him out of bed before he had truly woken up, otherwise he would hardly have gone to open the door, given that there was no reason for anyone to be looking for him there.

He was mistaken, though: at the door stood a postman who happened to be looking for "a certain Köves."

In his room, Köves immediatly opened the letter: it informed him that the editorial office of the newspaper on which he had been functioning up to that point as a journalist was hereby giving him notice of dismissal, and although, in compliance with the provisions of such and such a labour law, his salary would be paid to him for a further fortnight —"which may be collected at our cashier's desk during business hours on any working day"— they would be making no claims on his services from today's date onwards.

Köves read through the letter with a mixture of confusion, anger, and anxiety. How was this? Did life here begin with a person being dismissed from his job?

[…] The letter had turned him into a journalist, and more specifically a journalist who had been dismissed, so he had to follow up on that clue […].

Köves's victories Köves rushed for a tramcar; it was getting on for noon, so he might have missed the "business hours" mentioned in the dismissal letter; he found the stop easily, though it was not exactly in the place he had looked for it, the former traffic island now being just a pile of grey paving stones that had been thrown on top of one another, from which direction came the intermittent bursts of hammering of sluggishly moving road workers, but as to whether the road had been torn apart by bombs, or ripped up to form a barricade that was now being repaired, or was just being widened, Köves was in no position to know.

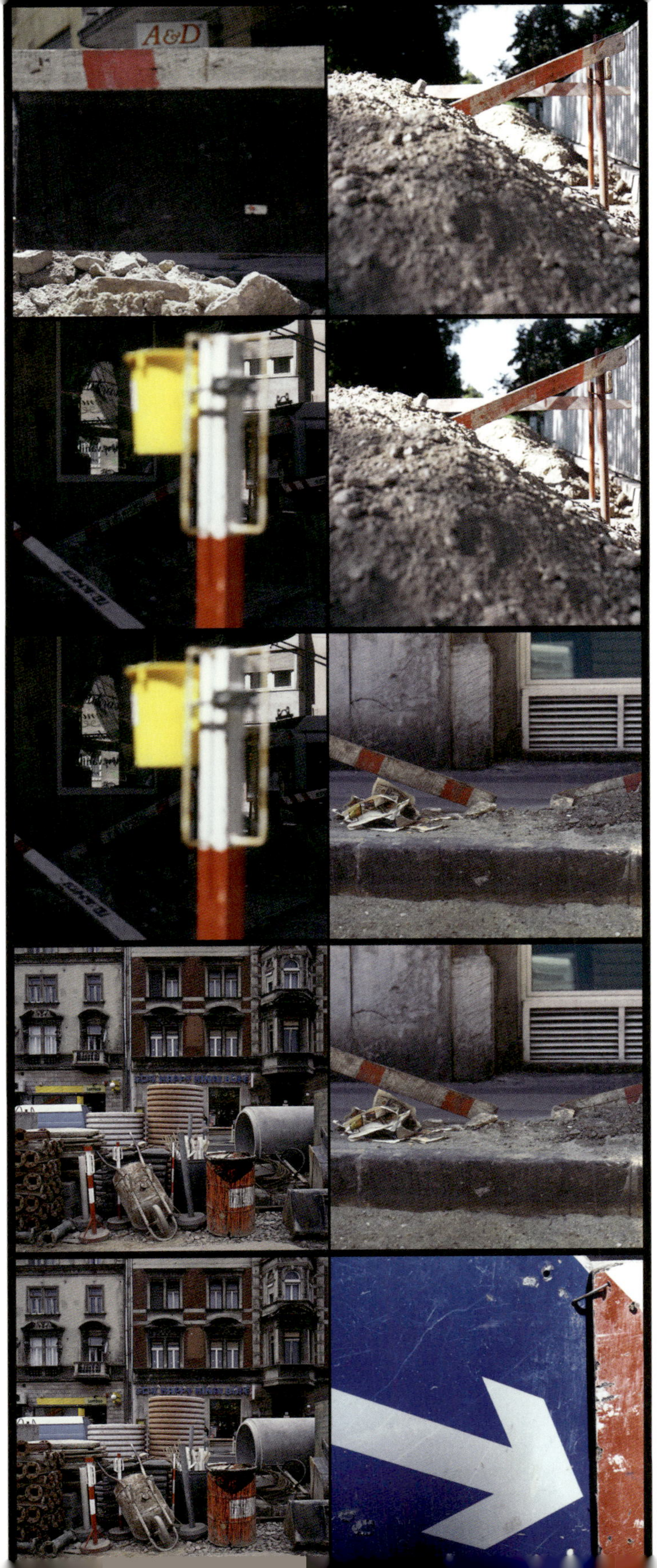
A&D

He had to face further difficulties at the entrance to the newspaper office: the doorkeeper, a customs man with holstered gun, was under no circumstances willing to let him in without an entry pass (Köves would hardly have said he was surprised, deep down he had expected there would be some sort of obstacle like this, except he had been thinking of later on, already imagining himself caught up in easygoing simple-mindedness at the cashier's desk) [...].

Although no one paid any attention to him any longer, he nevertheless felt that all eyes were fixed on him, and the filling-in of each new permit seemed as if it were not an entry into the building so much as serving solely for his—Köves's—further humiliation. At all events, there could be no doubting that without the necessary will, and the appropriate expression of that will, just like he failed to get on the tram, he was also not going to get into the newspaper office. The trouble being that in this respect Köves now found himself somewhat perplexed: he did not know what he was supposed to wish for.

[...] Because what he really wished for was something quite different, and that would have been a breakthrough into another realm, a break with all sanity: Köves wished quite simply to strike the porter's face, and to feel with his fists how the onetime face was pounded into a slushy, shapeless mush [...].

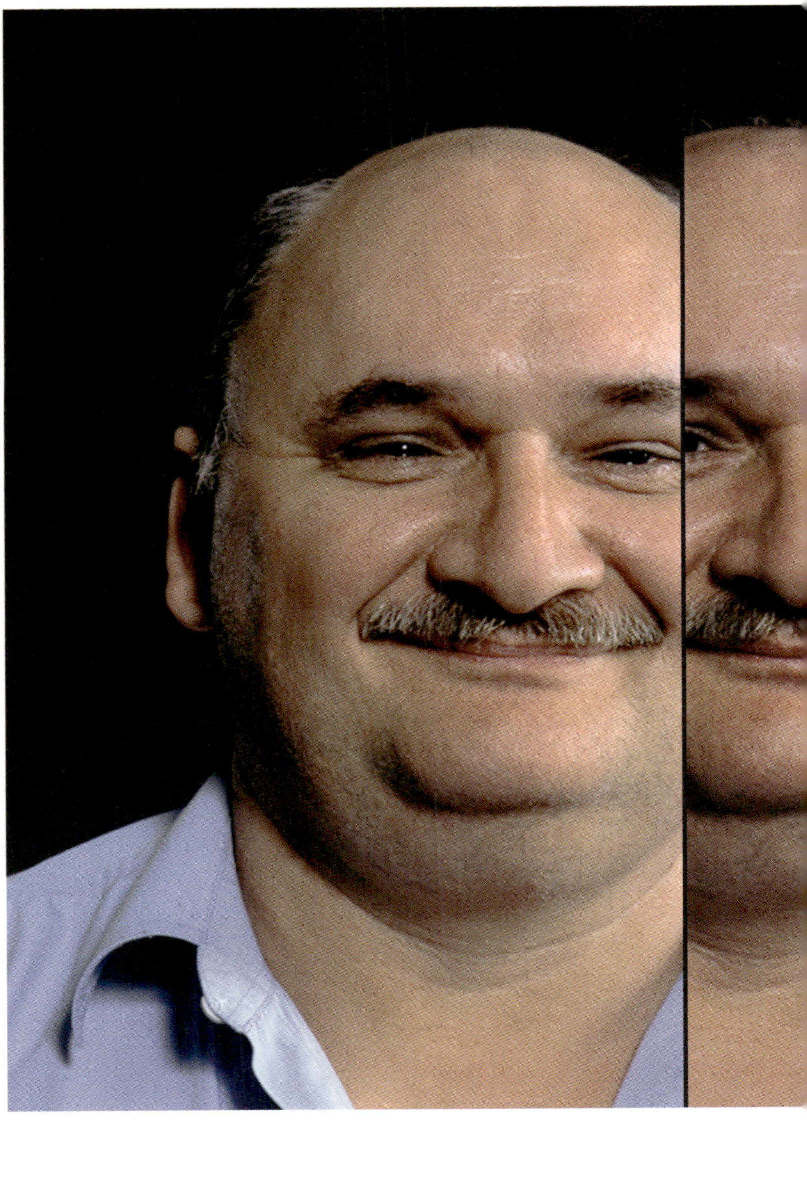

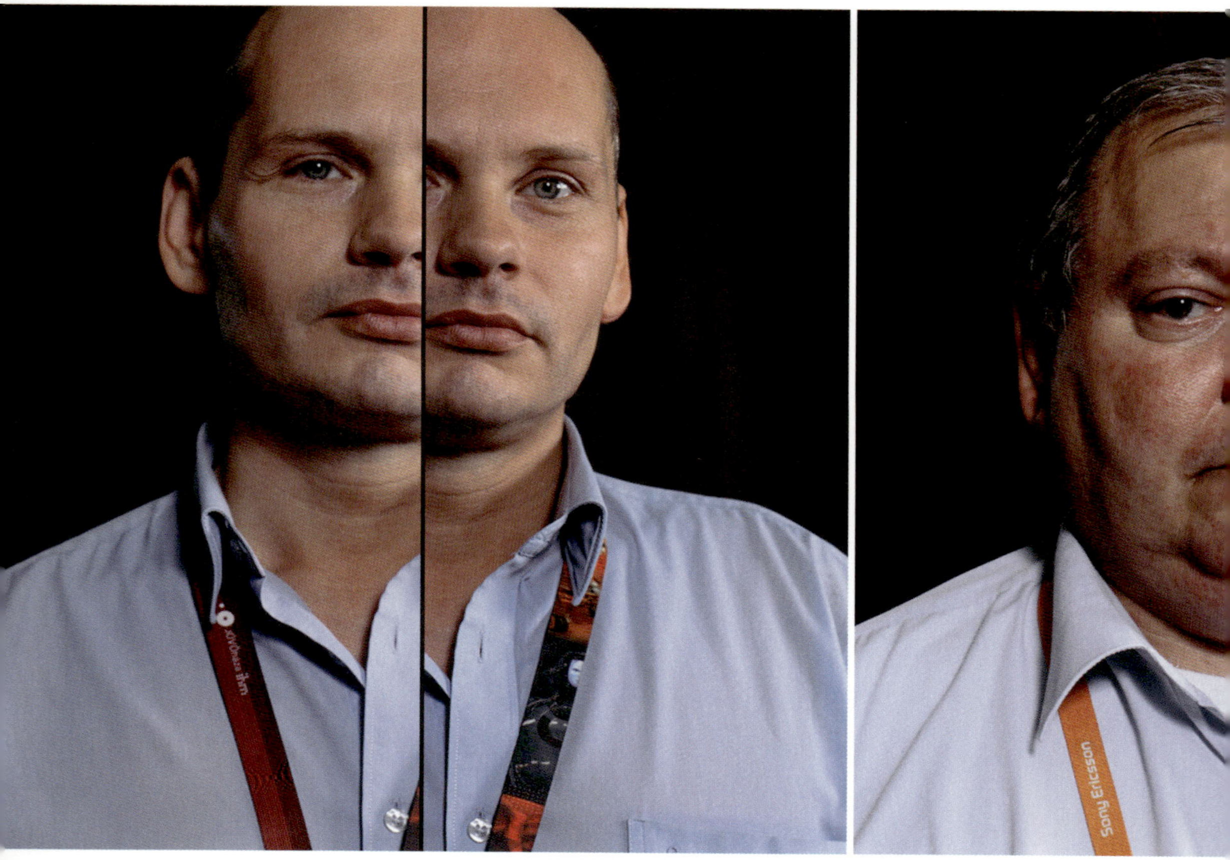
Sony Ericsson

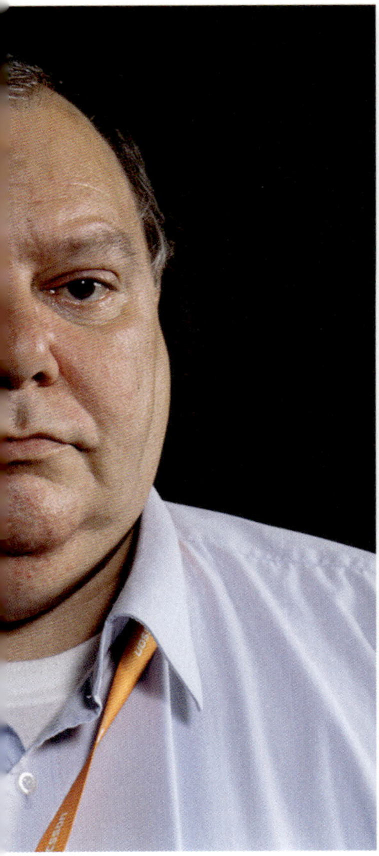

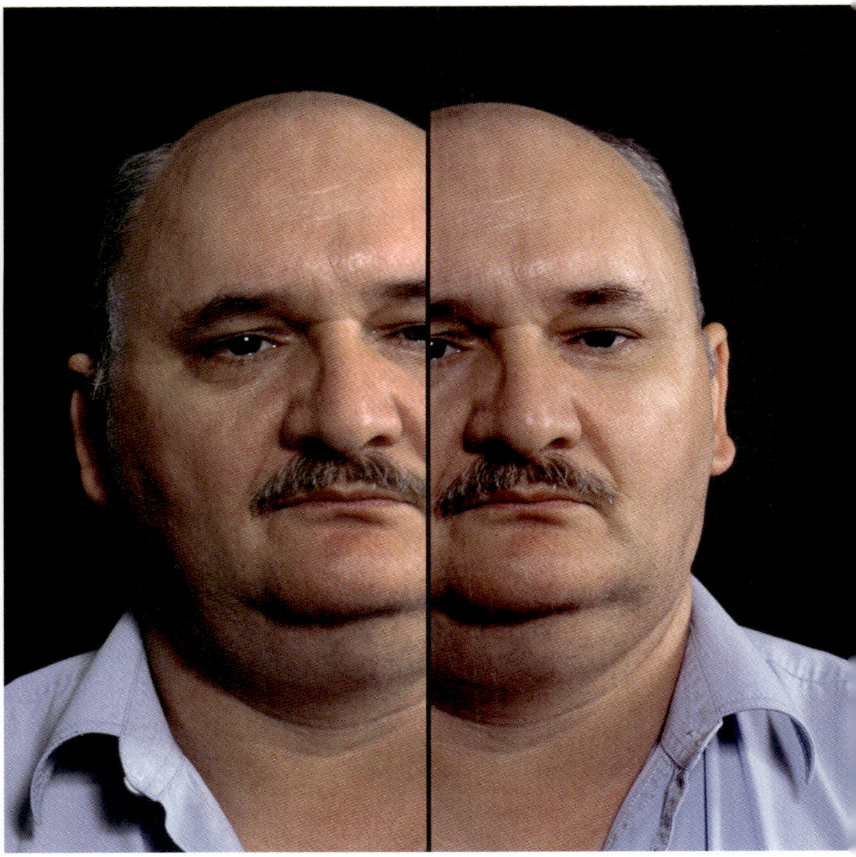

**Continuation
(a further victory)**   Köves felt dull and tired, his heart was hammering, his eyelids kept on listlessly closing as if the victory he had just gained had drained all his strength, although of course he was still in want of sleep and had also forgotten to eat breakfast. Was it always going to be like this? Would he always have to squeeze from himself such violent, self-tormenting passions each and every time he wished to move ahead? How was he going to control his emotions, and especially his sense of direction; after all, where was he actually headed? Which way was ahead?

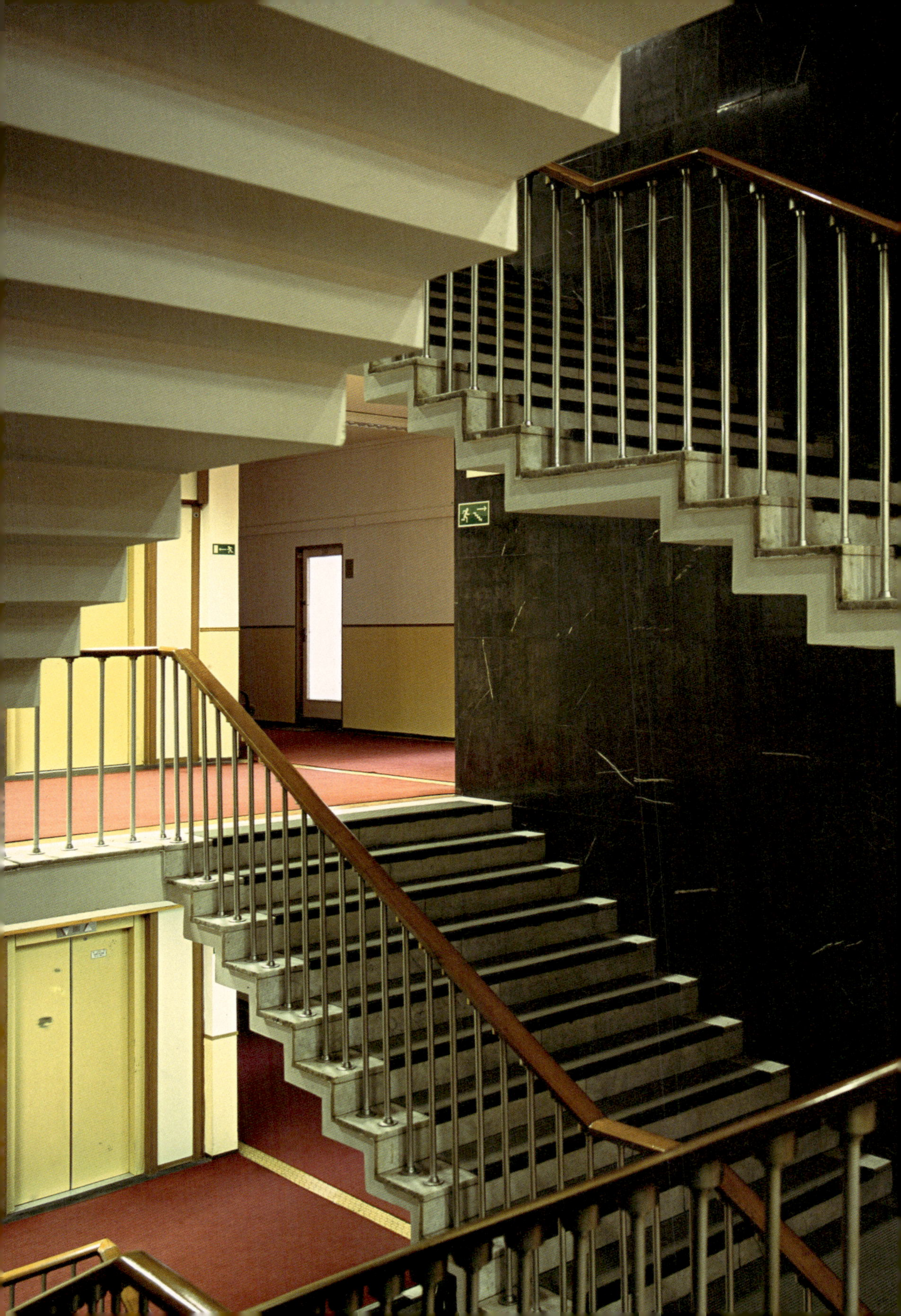

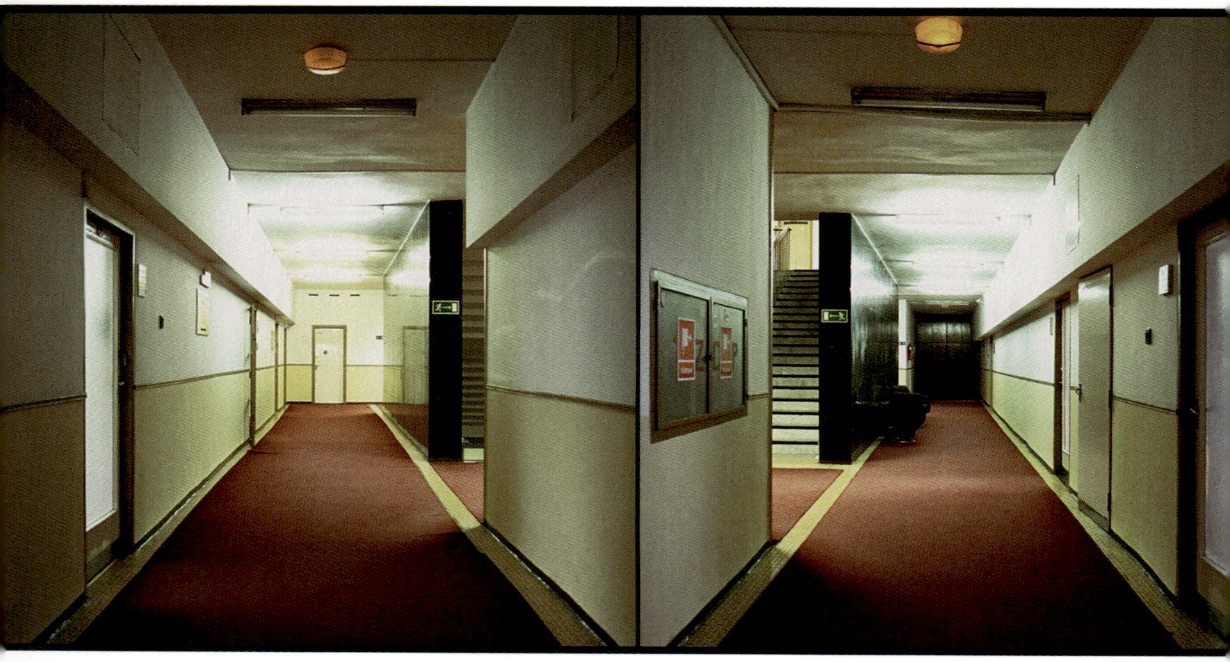

As per *Dossier K.*, from 1940–50 Imre Kertész was employed as a journalist with the daily newspaper *Világossag* (later called *Esti Budapest*) which was restructured after the communists took power and became the party organ for the Hungarian Communist Party. *Photos:* Former administration building of Ganz-MAVÀG (metalworking factory), today: *Gazdasag és közlekedesi Minisztérium* (Ministry for Economics and Transport), *Margit körút*.

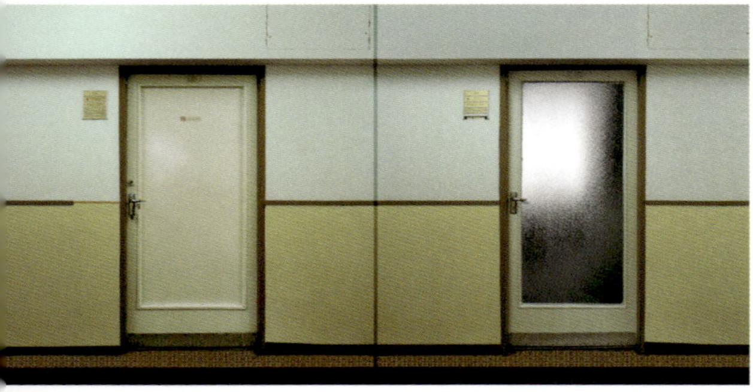
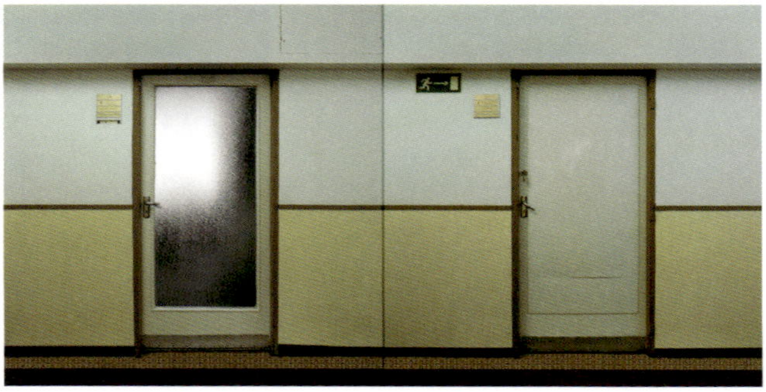
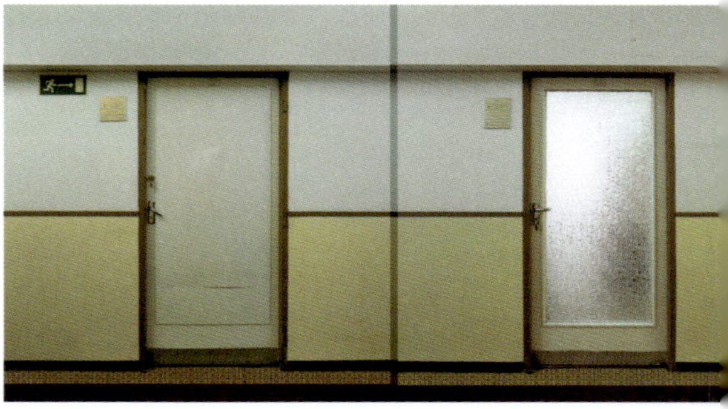
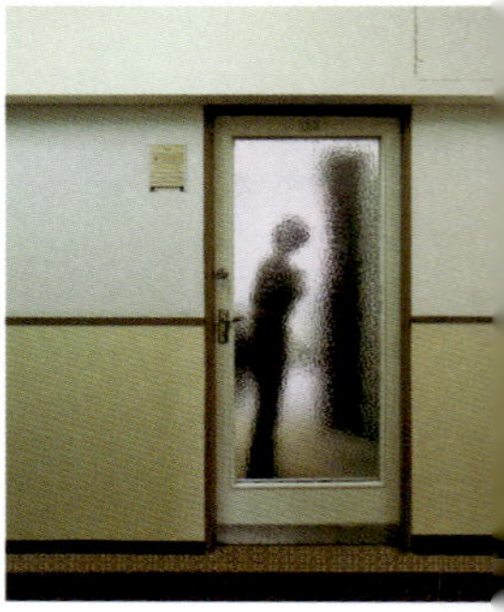

Continuation
(a yet further victory)

As he stepped through the double door, Köves at first saw virtually nothing, and even later only a little; in the daylight that streamed in through the wide window, literally stabbing and unremittingly pricking his eyes, which already stinging from lack of sleep, all he could see behind an enormous writing desk was a compact lacuna, a dark form hewn out of the light as it were, that was nevertheless arranged in accordance with the forms of a human trunk, shoulders, neck, and head—obviously the editor in chief.

"Naturally, you have to make a living; we all have to make a living." The head moved about while it was speaking, so that Köves was now slowly able to make out the outline of a jutting chin and a forceful, imperious nose. "But then, ultimately it's not a matter of prime importance."

"It becomes a matter of prime importance if you have nothing to live off of," said Köves.

"Everyone in our country makes a living," and now Köves sensed in the voice something final, brooking no denial, as if he had been put in his place. "As far as your dismissal goes," the editor in chief went on, now with a somewhat more expansive intonation, "we weighed it up meticulously. To tell you the truth, we can't really see how we could make use of you."

Köves tried to collect his thoughts as a suspicion was aroused in him that he was walking into a trap. "I can formulate proper grammatical sentences. I'm skilled at rounding out a story and supplying a punch line…maybe," he added with a modest, self-deprecating smile, as if he wished to avoid the appearence of bragging, "well anyway, perhaps I also have some style."

"And you have no credo…no persuasion?" and Köves suddenly felt like someone sizing up the depths of a chasm—and quite irrationally, too, since if he were going to jump, he would do better to jump with his eyes closed.

"Life is not a source of faith, after all, life is … I don't know what, but life is something else…"

He was soon interrupted:

"You're not familiar with the life we lead."

"I'd like to work, and then I shall get to know it," Köves said, in a low voice now, almost longingly.

"You'll learn: our factories are waiting with open gates for anyone who wishes to work!" chimed the voice, and Köves lifted his head again: the recognition, like a judgement, filled him with a calm, dull weariness, but in it he somehow regained his keen sense of pride.

South Seas   […] On getting out onto the corridor he passed a man who, Köves remembered, had happened to be picking up some money immediately before him at the cashier's desk and was just in the process of counting the bank notes yet again, for he too was visibly not very satisfied with the amount. As Köves went past, without raising his head, the man asked:

"They've kicked you out too?"

"Yep," said Köves […].

"They sent you off into the country, and by the time you returned, the notice of dismissal was waiting for you, right?"

"Right," Köves admitted.

"That's what they usually do," the other nodded. "We got out of it rather well," he added, as he and Köves stepped together into one of the descending boxes, which carried on sinking with them as its load.

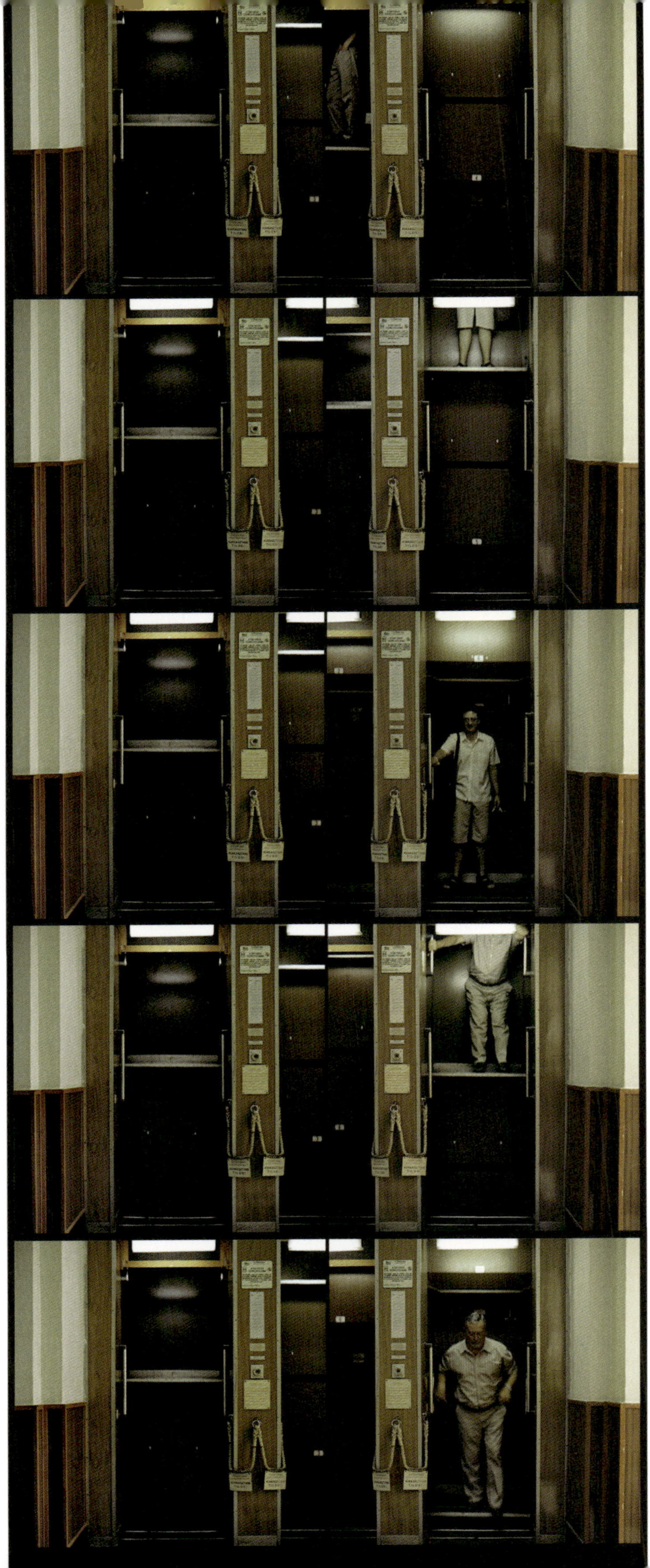

[…] The sunlight, the traffic, even the scanty, small-town bustle worked on Köves, with his all-accommodating and equalizing indifference, rather like an act of kindness. "These recent changes…," the previous voice caught his ear, and Köves snatched up his head in surprise: he had already forgotten that he was not alone.

"What changes?" he asked, more just out of politeness, as he had a shrewd idea in advance that the answer would be exactly what it was:

"Can anyone know?"

"No, they can't." Köves nodded, feeling that he was taking part with obligatory automatism in some ceremony then in fashion.

But then something came to mind, this time a genuine question, touching on the heart of the matter, which he really ought to have addressed to himself but which he posed to the other all the same:

"So, what are you going to do now?" […]

"We'll go to the South Seas, you can always get something there."

Washing of waves   When he had drifted in through the old-fashioned, glazed revolving door, it suddenly seemed to Köves that he was both aquainted with the place—a vast barn of a room, divided up into two or maybe more interconnecting spaces—and then again not, but at all events time had not passed by even the South Seas without leaving its mark: the velvet drapery showed signs of wear, a solitary piano on the podium, forlorn and shrouded in a cover—the whole thing gave the overall picture of a diner and coffee bar, gambling den and daytime refuge which had started to go downhill, where his new friend, Sziklai—on hearing the name something flashed through Köves's mind, nothing more than a vague memory in a world where the vagueness of memories vies with that of the present—plainly felt completely at home […].

[…] Köves took in only a fraction of what he said about them. Regarding a fat, balding man, whose sickly-coloured face, despite the occasional mopping with a handkerchief as big as a bedsheet, was constantly glistening with perspiration and whose table seemed to be a sort of focal point, at which people arrived in a hurry, then settled for a while before jumping up again, whereas others stayed there for longer exchanges of ideas, a person whom Sziklai himself also greeted (the bald man cordially returned the nod), Köves found out that he was the "Uncrowned," and although who gave him that nickname was unclear, its import was easy to explain because he was the uncrowned king there, with half the coffee bar working just for him, Sziklai recounted.

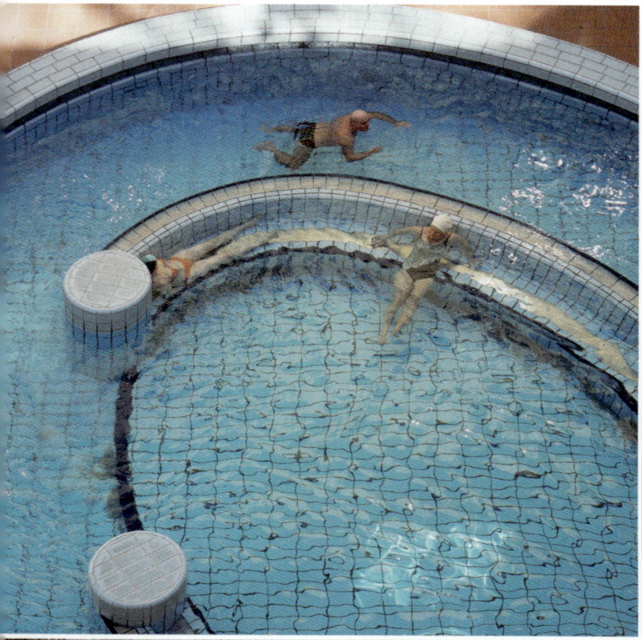
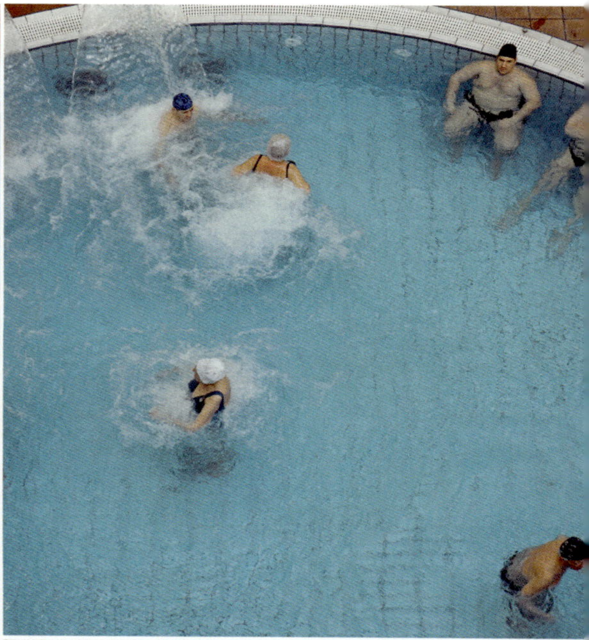
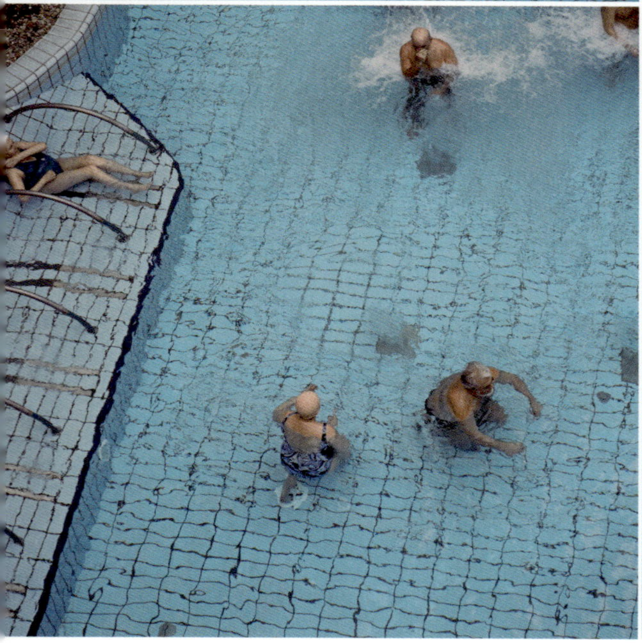
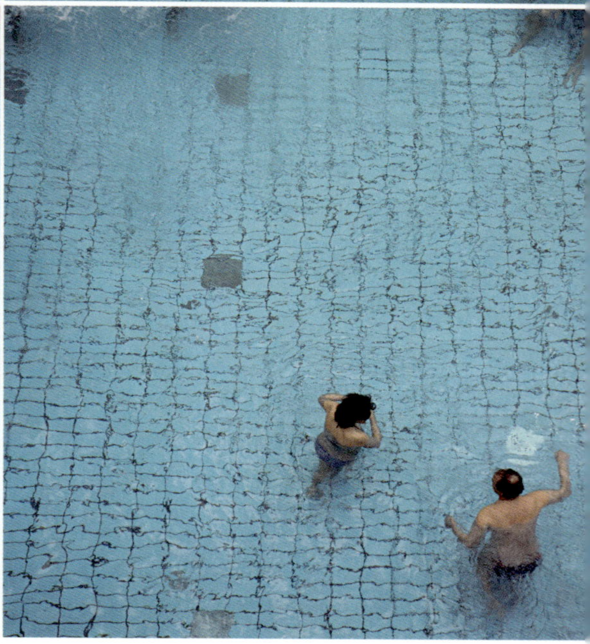

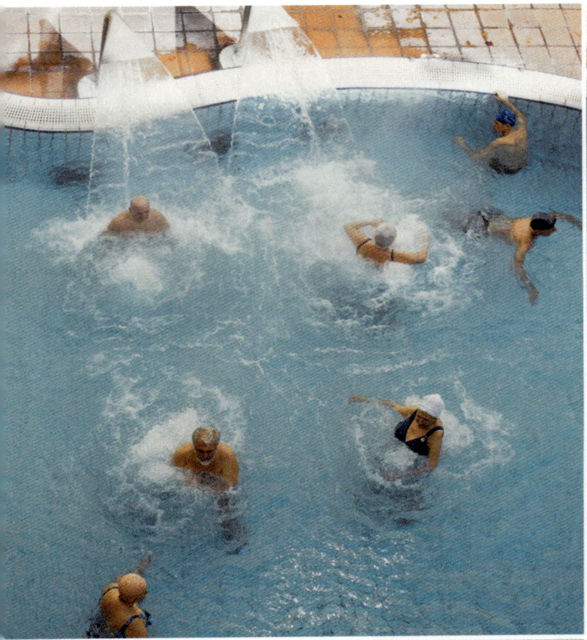
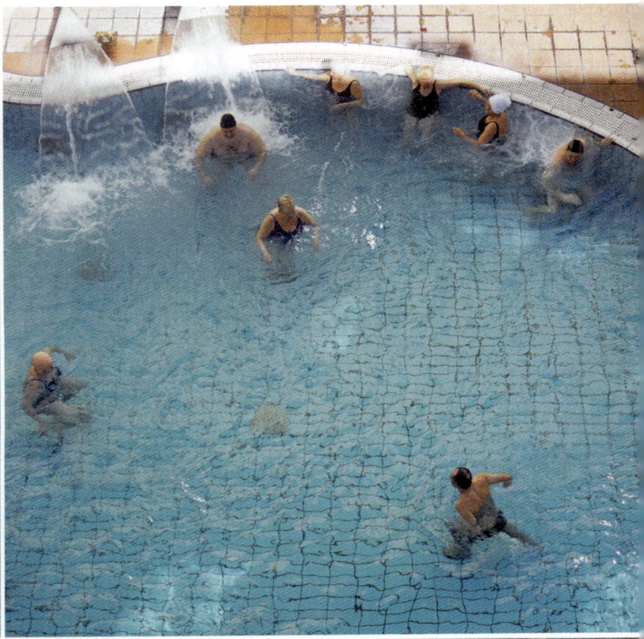
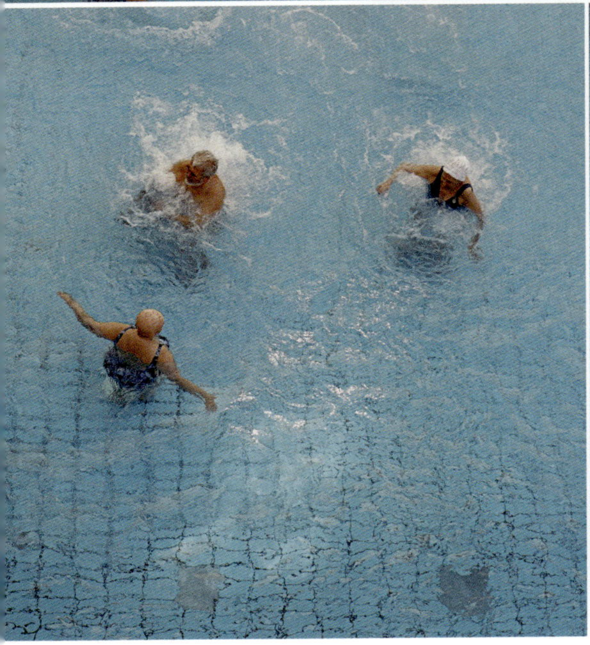
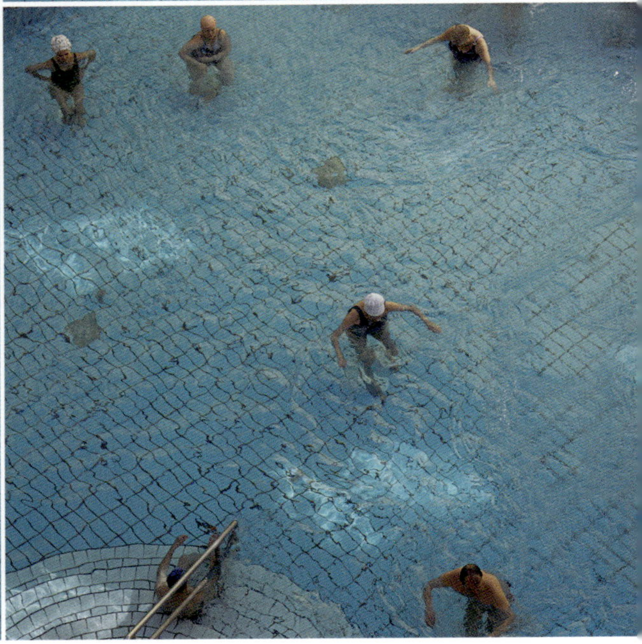

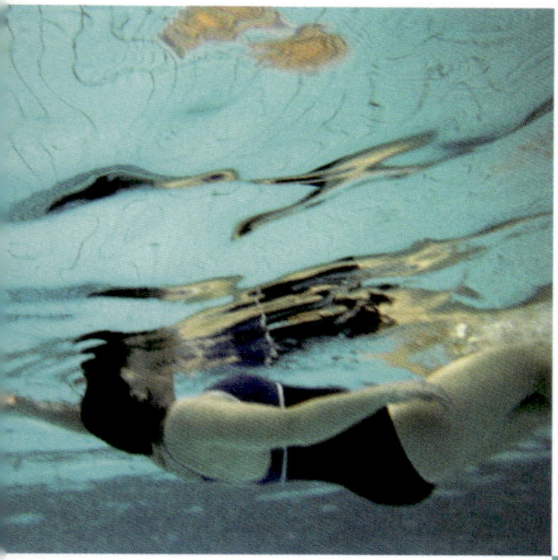
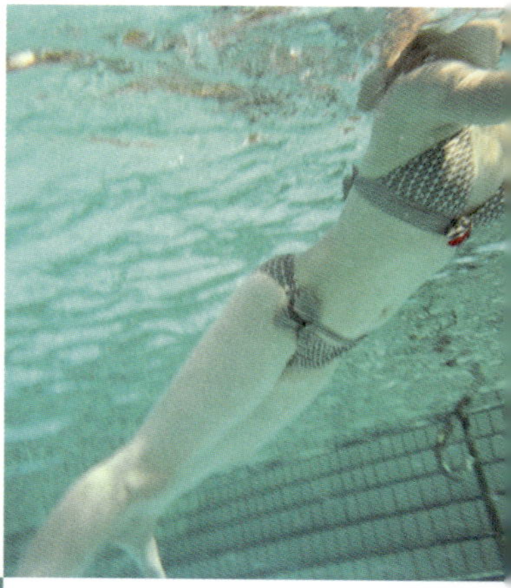
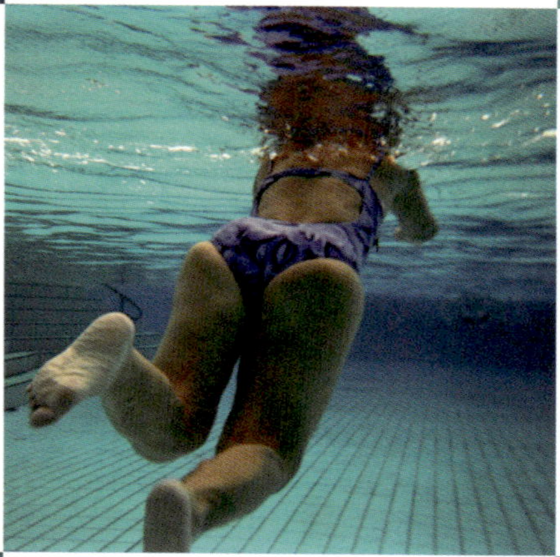
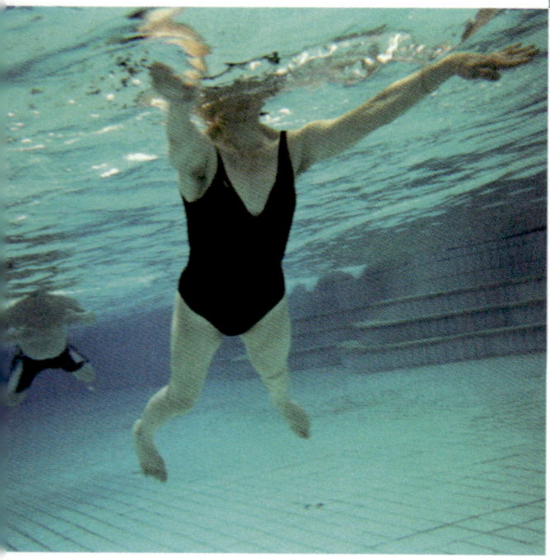
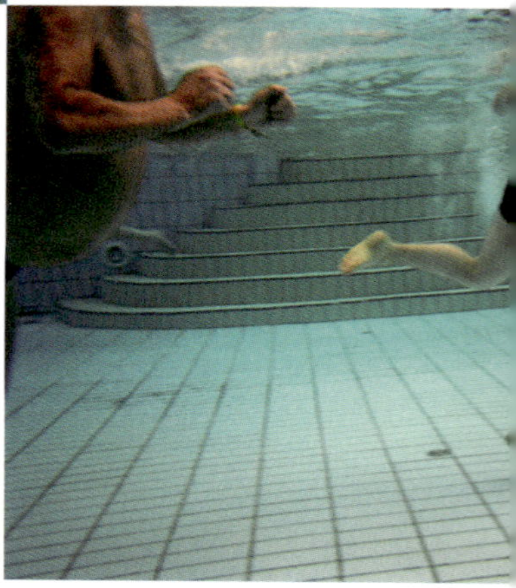

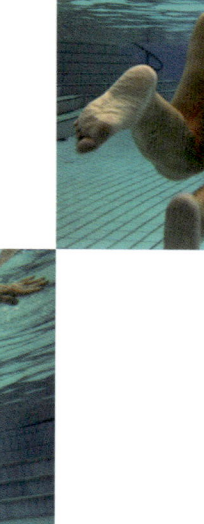

Also, there were plenty of people who needed "papers," said Sziklai. That was how they would come to be working for the Uncrowned: one way or another, he would obtain an official document for them, which stated that they were working for a non-profit company. That way they would not be open to charges of workshyness or sponging [...].

"We'll get by somehow," said Sziklai looking pensively at Köves. "There are two ways," he went on: "the short and narrow, which leads nowhere, then the long and roundabout way, which leads to who knows where, but at least one has the sense of moving ahead. You should bear that in mind," he added promptly with a touch of careladen anxiety […]. "I reckon it needs to be a light comedy: that's what will bring success."

"Success?" Köves questioned, hesitantly, as if he were getting his mouth round a strange, near-unpronounceable word in a foreign language.

"Of course," Sziklai looked at him impatiently. "One has to make a success of something. Success is the only way out."

"Out of what?"

.

The photographs of the "South Seas" (probably the restaurant *Abázia* in the novel and today a bank) were shot in *Lukács fürdő* and *Széchenyi fürdő* (two thermal baths). At the start of the 1960s, Imre Kertész usually went to *Lukács fürdő* in the evenings. The thermal baths had become increasingly popular meeting places for artists and intellectuals as it was not possible to listen to what was being said there thanks to the lapping and splashing of the water.

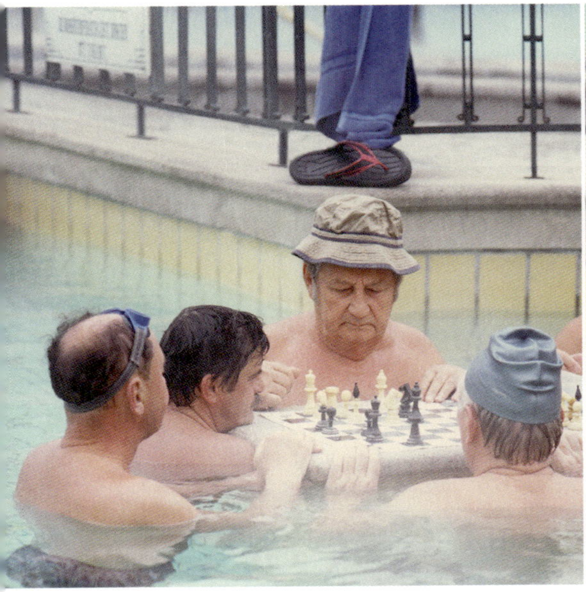
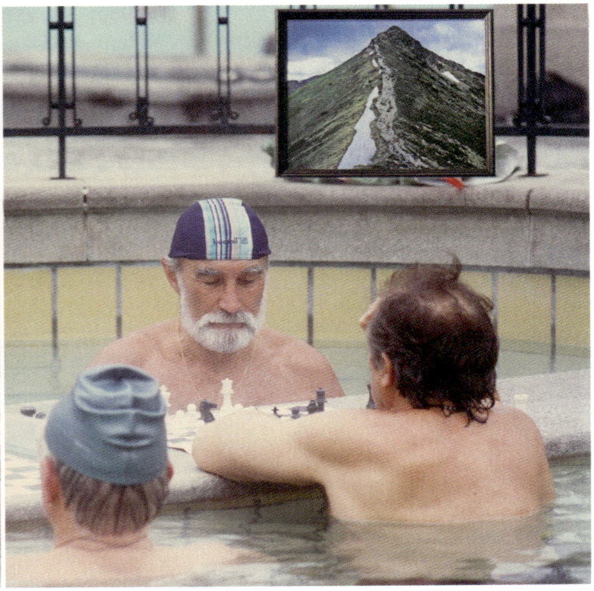
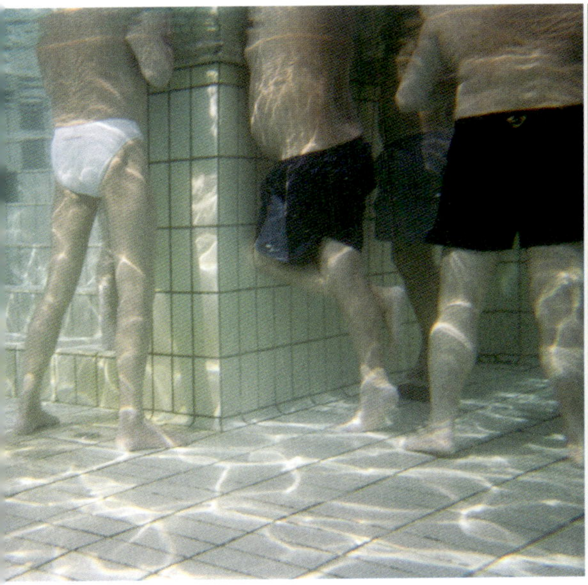
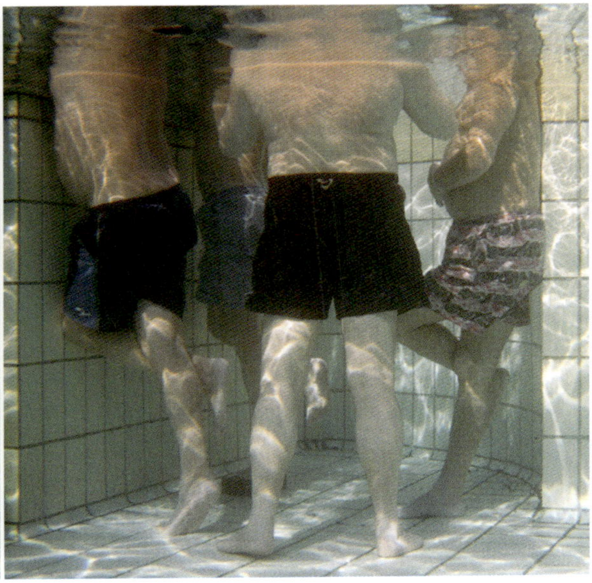

The South Seas: a strange acquaintance

"Berg!"—snippily, sternly, and yet somehow still sonorously: it was already known to Köves, of course, along with the usual dismissive waves of the hand and expressions of commiseration accorded Alice by common consent, whenever the South Seas' regulars mentioned the name—if it was mentioned at all—among themselves.

"Journalist?" he asked.

"Yes," said Köves. "But I've been fired," he added promptly, to preempt any possible misunderstandings as it were.

"Well, well!" Berg remarked. "Why was that?"

To which Köves, breaking into a smile, responded:

"Can anyone know?"

"One can," Berg said resolutely in his high voice. So that Köves, plainly surprised by an answer of the sort which was so uncommon there, said, shrugging his shoulders with a slightly forced lightheartedness:

"Then it appears you know more than I, because I don't know, that's for sure."

"But of course you know," said Berg, seemingly annoyed by the contradiction. "Everybody knows; at most they pretend to be surprised," and here a distant memory was suddenly awakened in Köves, as if he had already heard something similar here before [...].

"Could it be that you too were kicked out?" he asked, because he seemed to recall having heard something of the kind about Berg, though he did not remember precisely, of course, for in the South Seas, as Köves had begun to notice bit by bit, people knew everything about everybody and nothing about anybody.

It seemed, though, that Berg, too, was sparing with accurate information:

"You could put it like that," […].

"And"—it went against his practice, but this time Köves, for some reason, did not wish to concede the point — "do you know why?"

"Of course I do," Berg said coolly, resolutely, indeed even raising his eyebrows slightly as though exasperated by Köves's obtuseness. "Because I was found to be unsuitable."

"But what are you suited for?" Köves kept plugging away.

"You see," Berg's face now assumed a ruminative expression, not looking at Köves, almost as though he were not talking to him but to himself: "that's the point. Probably for everything. Or to be more precise, anything. No matter. Presumably I was afraid to give it a try," and, returning to the real world as it were, Berg now looked around the table with a searching gaze until his eyes alighted on the serviettes, on one of which he proceeded to wipe his fingers, which were clearly sticky from the petits fours. "And now we shall never know," he continued, "because I have been excluded from the decision-making domain." […].

"They seem to have forgotten about me."

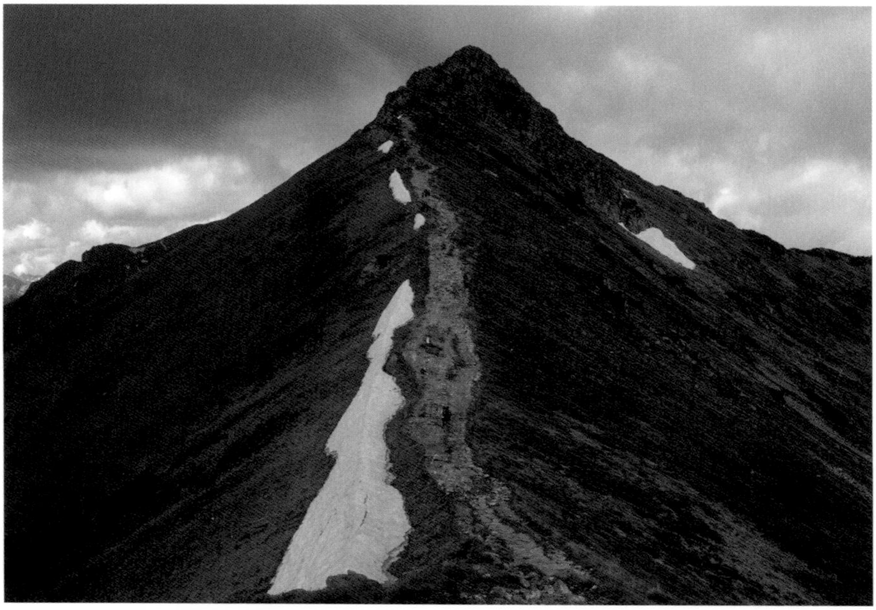

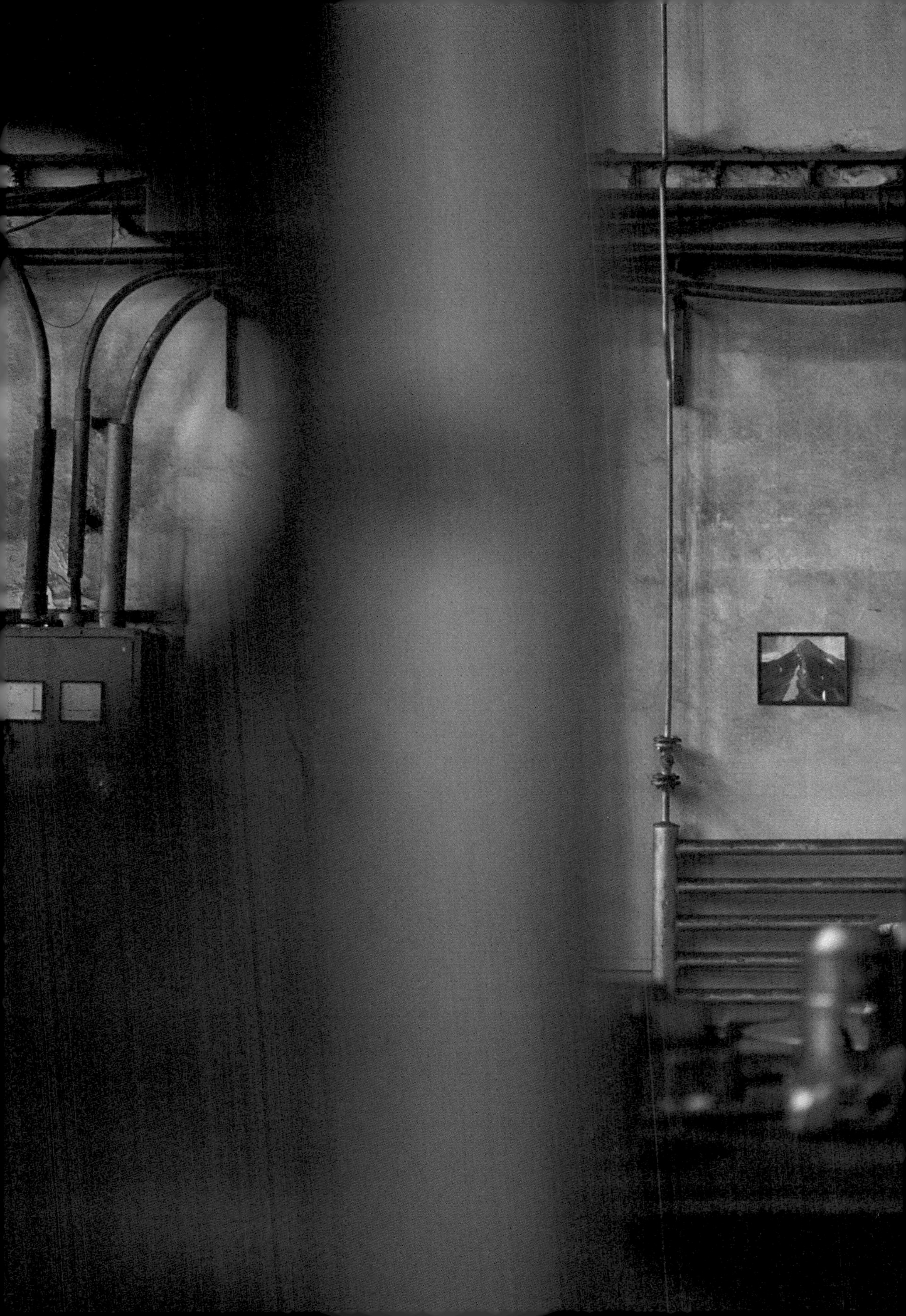

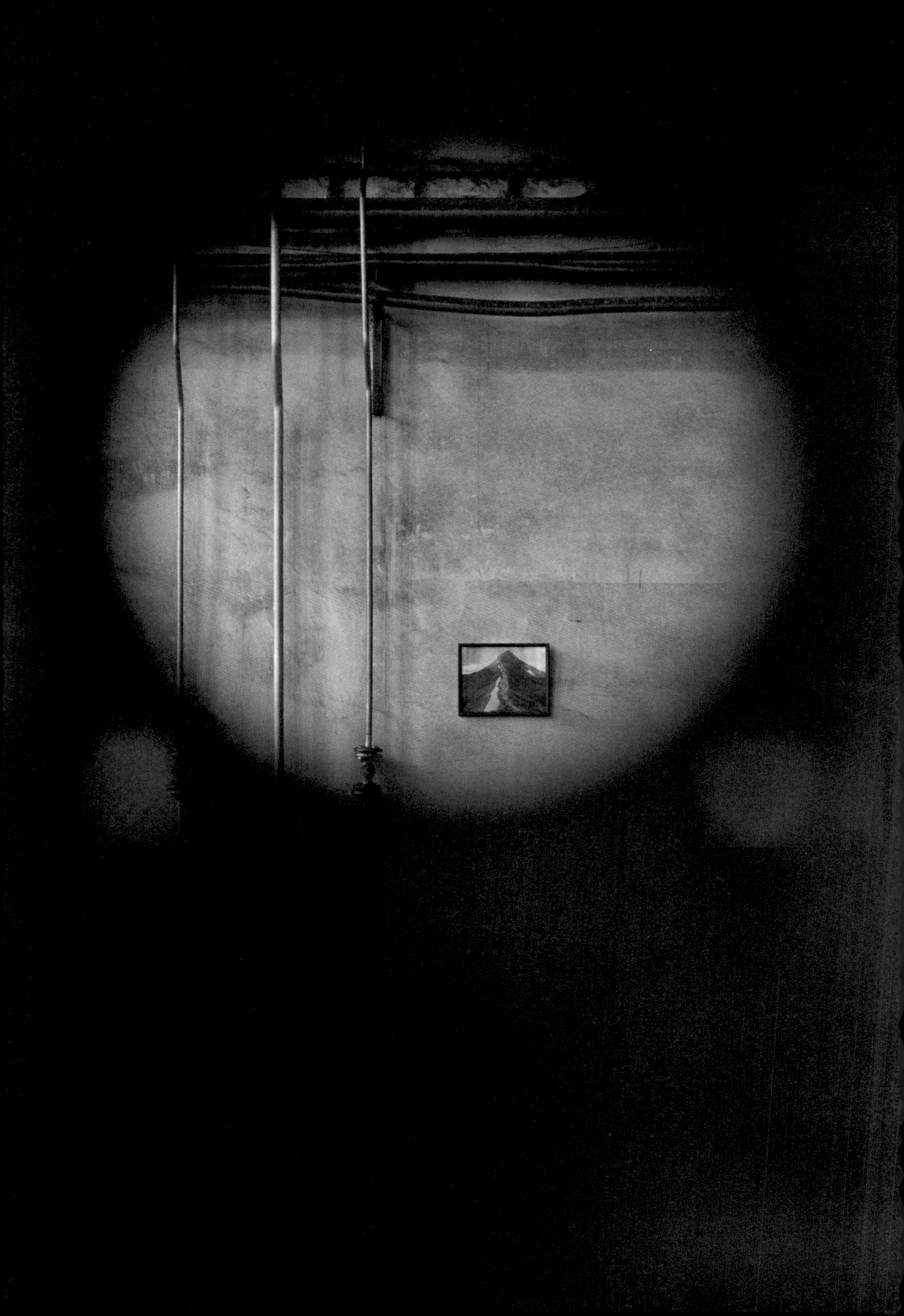

Accident. Girlfriend   [...] The factories in the city were mostly steelworks, and a steelworks devours manpower, so they were always taking people on, and at the employment office Köves was advised to sign on as a machine fitter. Köves was none too eager, on the grounds that if there were fitters, what was the point of a machine fitter, why not a locksmith, who — Köves imagined—produced locks, keys, fastenings, that kind of thing [...].

It soon became clear, though, that this was the only opening on offer at the employment office: what had been brought to Köves's attention at his first word, as a piece of good advice, proved, as such, to be more of a command for him [...].

As can be found in *Dossier K.*, in January 1951 Kertész was given notice of dismissal in accordance with the regulations from the newspaper publisher *Szikra Könyvkiadó* (The Spark). He was obliged to find another position within three months so as not to be charged under the "unwilling to work, danger to the common good" regulation and got a job as a factory worker in MÁVAG (Hungarian State Railroad Machine Factory). Photos: *Go metall Kft.* from the former premises of the *Csepel Vas-és Femművek* (Csepel Iron and Metal Works).

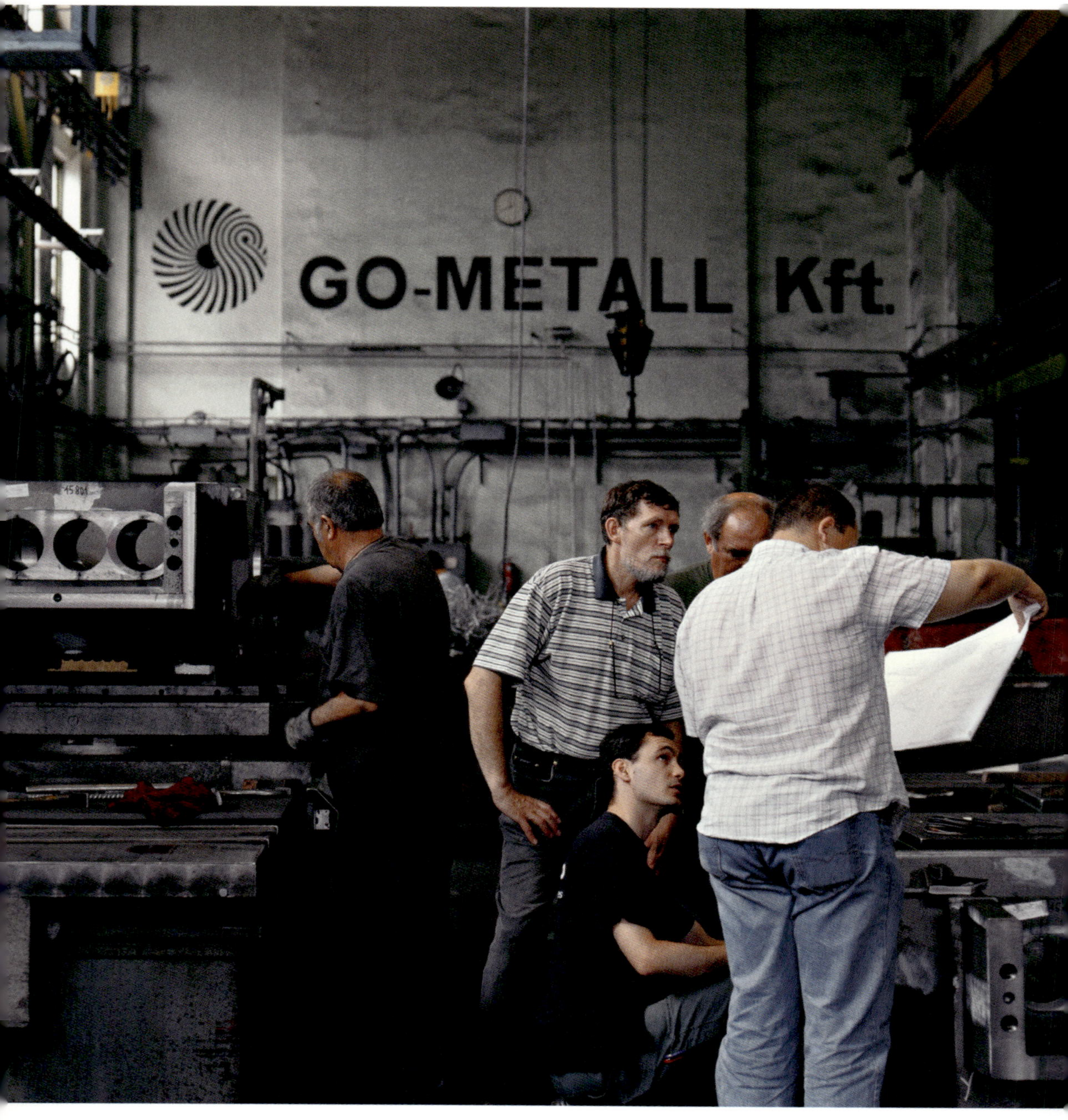
GO-METALL Kft.

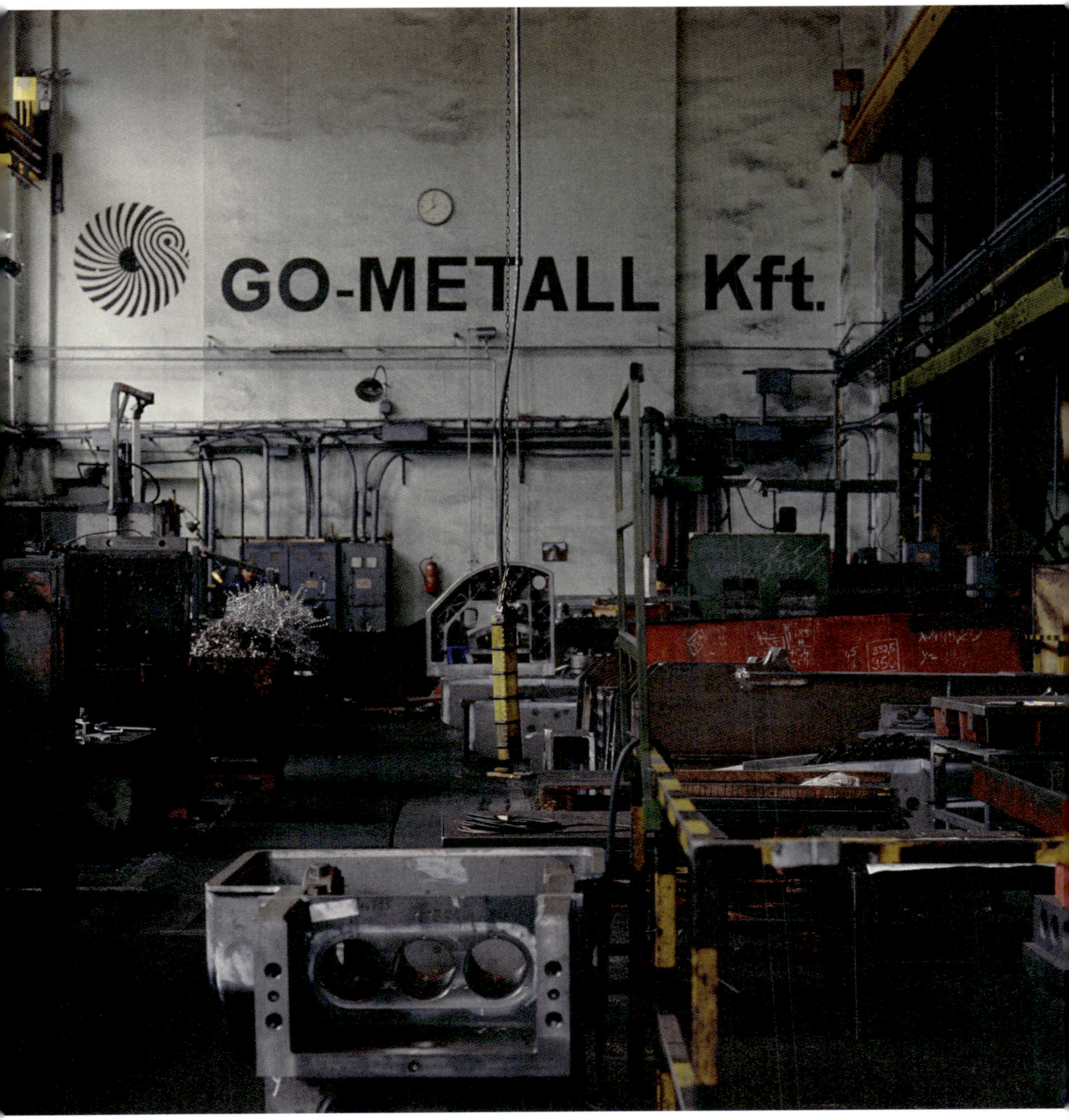
GO-METALL Kft.

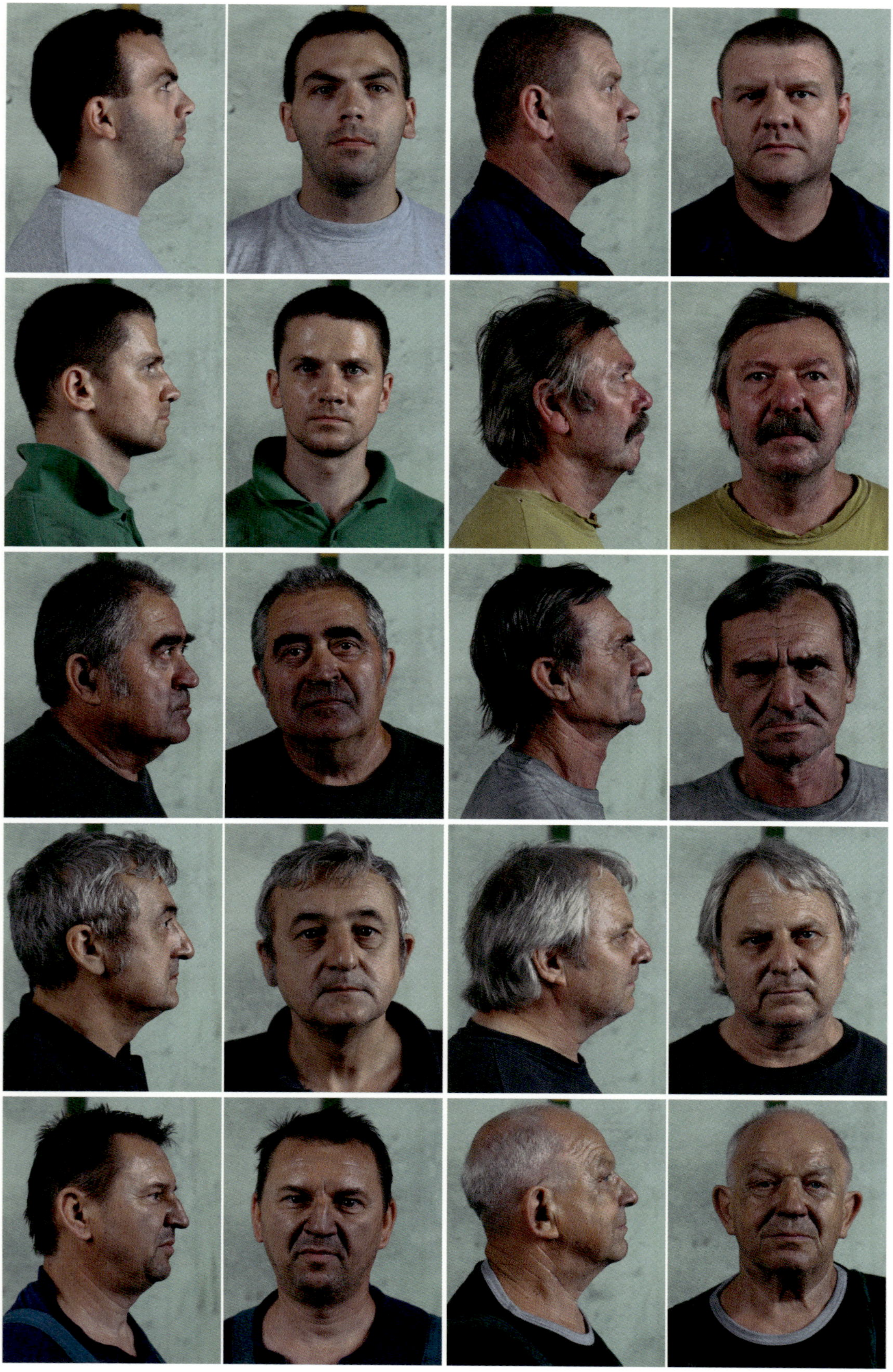

[…] The people around Köves learning the machine-fitting craft were all adults, some learning for one reason, some for another (in most cases the exact reason never emerged, and making enquiries, for which Köves had neither the time nor the inclination, seemed to be frowned on there), but in any event next to Köves a slim man with a moustache and a pleasant outward appearance was filing, engrossed in his work and silently, in shirtsleeves and a peaked cap of a kind that at most Köves might have seen abroad, had he been interested in equestrian sports, as well as gloves that an expert eye would have been able to recognize, despite the wear and tear, the stains and holes, as being made of buckskin. Had he been fired from somewhere? Or was some guilt burdening his conscience (like Köves's, too, in all probability), and had he become a machine fitter as a punishment or, for that matter, out of clemency? Or had he perhaps originally had an occupation which had now simply lost relevance, become unnecessary, like that of the sluggish, slightly burly figure who was filing away a bit farther off, whose closer friends would sometimes, within earshot, call "Mr. Counsellor?" Köves had no way of knowing.

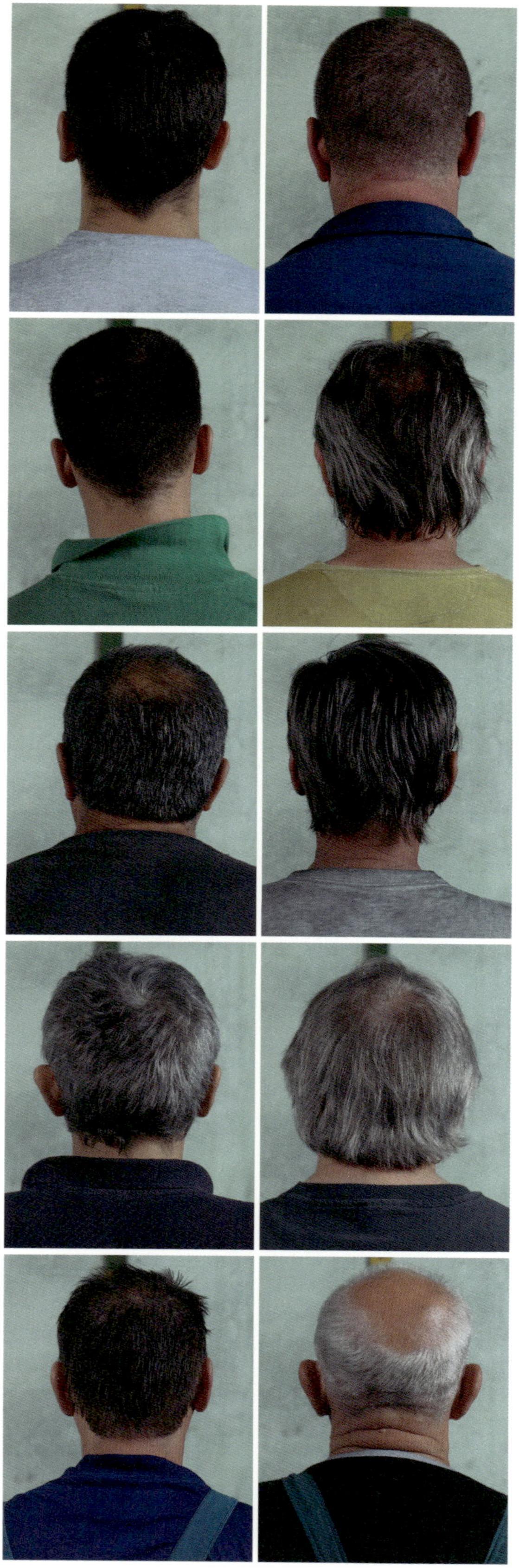

At other times, he would fasten his gaze on a pair of identical men — at any event both were stocky and balding, both were wearing brand-new blue overalls, which in Köves's eyes unaccountably looked like the external mark of some resolve, not unlike new penitents who don a monk's cowl yet, out of old habit, still get it made by their own tailor, filed away with dour assiduity: they were there in the morning, they disappeared in the evening, and they spoke not a word either to others or to each other; Köves heard that they had been dismissed from somewhere, but they considered that this had been a blunder and were now waiting as machine fitters for light to be cast on that blunder, and the reason they were so guarded was that they were afraid a fresh blunder might befall them, or even that they themselves might commit one.

In short, Köves was making do there (to some extent, being present as if he was not present at all, or as if it was not he who was present) [...].

Köves is summoned. Forced to have second thoughts

"Did you think you would be able to hide from us?! Tell me frankly, are you really satisfied here?!" at which Köves, who had been fidgeting on the seat in growing astonishment, was genuinely stunned. What was this? Was this a joke? [...] (He had not come to the steelworks in order to be satisfied, after all); but now he was being asked, even if it was hardly in all seriousness of course, and possibly was even expected to answer—for which he would still remain in their debt, of course —Köves felt that the entire time he had spent there was a single day, with its mornings and evenings maybe, but still a single, long, monotonous day, running constantly in the grey colours of dawn, that he kept scraping away at with his file as at an unerodable piece of steel [...].

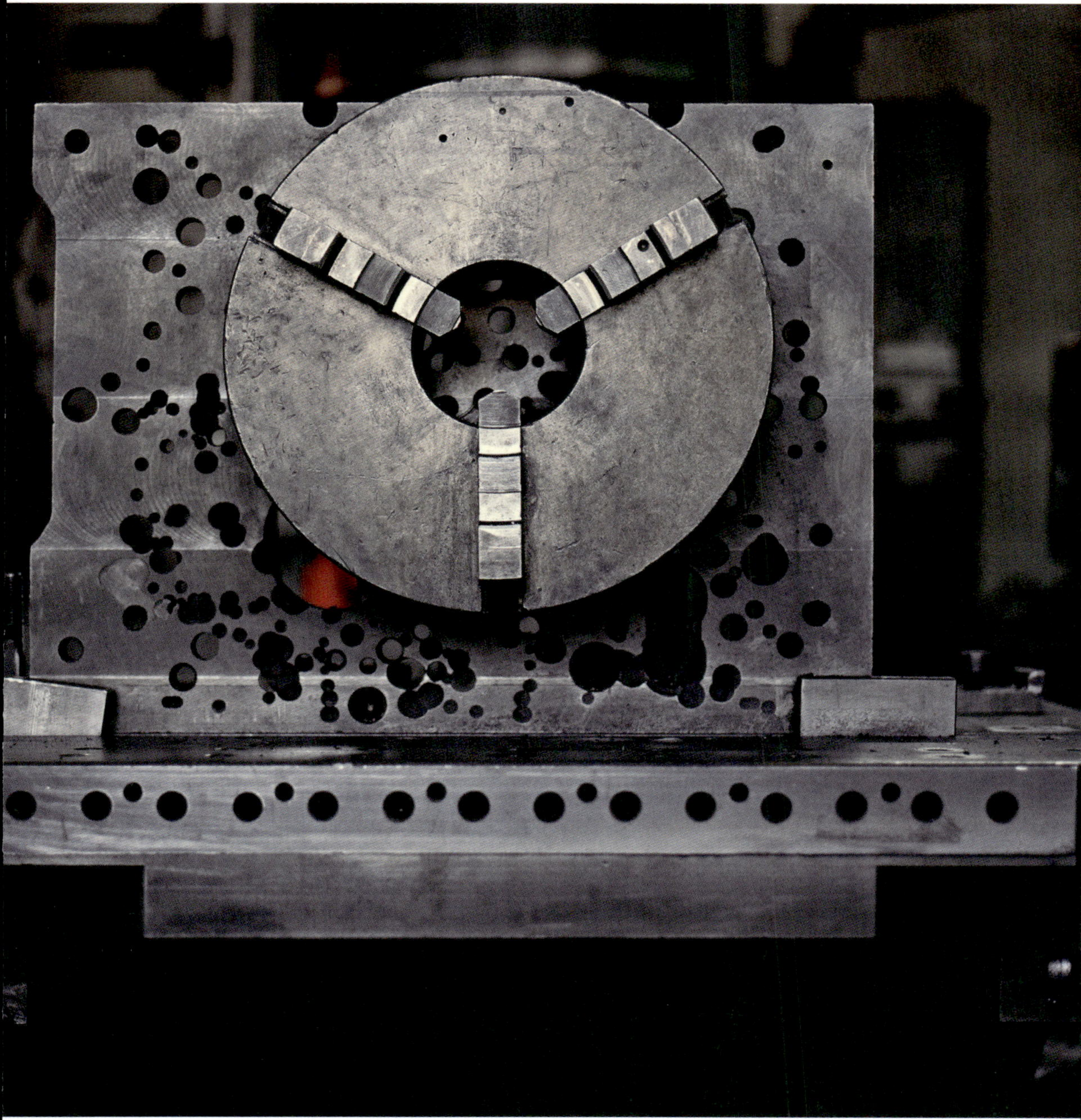

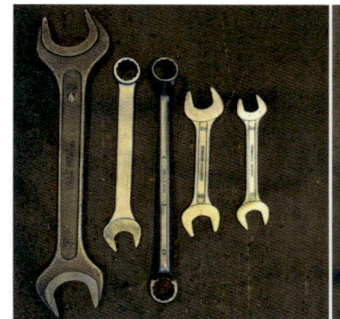

"You're a journalist. From tomorrow you'll be working for the press department of the Ministry of Production, the ministry which supervises us," and he had maybe not even got the words out, or Köves heard them, when, slipping out of Köves, brusquely and harshly, as if his life were under threat, came a:

"No!"

"No?" the department head leaned over the desk toward Köves, his face unexpectedly softening and sagging, his mouth opening slightly, his eyes staring confusedly at Köves from under the cap: "What do you mean, 'No'?" he asked, so Köves, who by then had visibly regained his poise, although this seemed to have reinforced rather than shaken his determination, repeated:

"No," like someone shielding something tangible against some kind of fantasy. And so as not to appear like the sort of uncounth bumpkin who could not even speak, he added by way of an explanation:

"I'm unsuited for it." [...].

"Who could know what he's suited for and what not? How many tests do we have to go through until it becomes clear who we are?" The department head was warming to the task, gradually bringing the colour of more briskly circulating blood to his pallid features. "Upstairs," and at this point the hand which, just before, had been reaching forward was now raised, fingers spread, as if he were raising a chalice above his head, "in higher circles, they've come to a decision about you."

"We are servants, servants, each and every one of us! I'm a servant, and you're a servant too. Is there anything more uplifting than that, more marvellous than that?"

"Whose servants?" Köves got a word in.

"Of a higher conceptualization," came the answer.

"And what is that conceptualization," Köves got in quickly, as if he were hoping he might finally learn something.

The question must have been over-hasty, however, because the department head stared mutely at him, as if he could not believe what he was hearing, and then he again glanced at the document that he was warming under his palm:

"Of course," he spoke finally. "You've returned home from abroad."

All the same, he answered the question Köves had asked, though by now in a much drier tone:

"Unbroken perfectionism."

"And of what does that consist?" Köves, seeming to have already accepted that he was a journalist once again, yet was not to be deflected.

"Our trying ceaselessly to put people to the test." The department head at this point indicated, with a brusque flip of the hand, that they had exhausted the subject and should revert to practical matters. "Consider it a piece of good luck," he said, "that you've been noticed," and it seemed that his words had a sudden sobering effect on Köves as well.

"I don't want good luck," he said, now in the same dry, determined tone and with a feeling he had already said that before to someone, even if then he may have been even less well-armed against luck than he was now. "I want to be a worker," he went on, "a good worker."

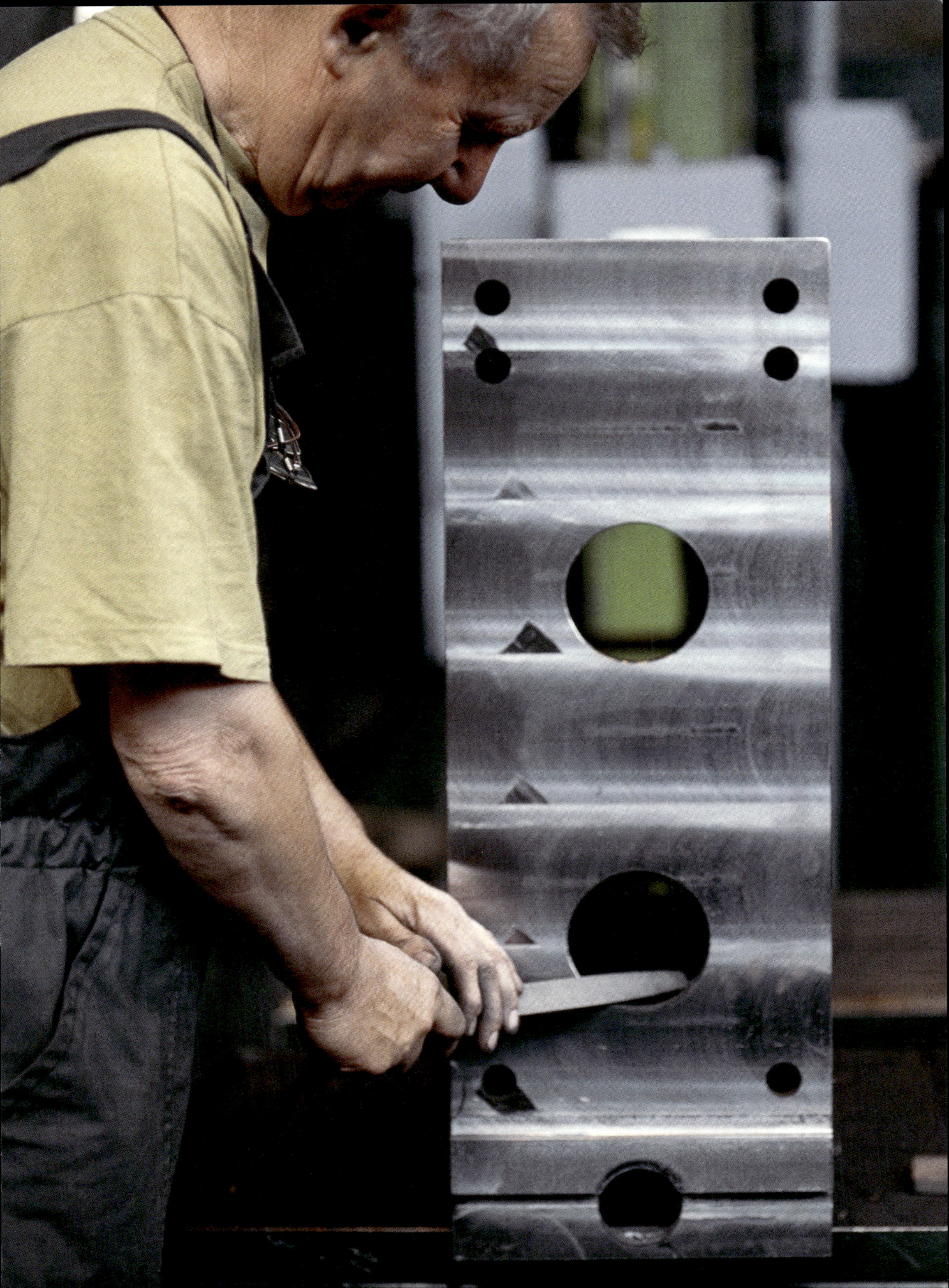

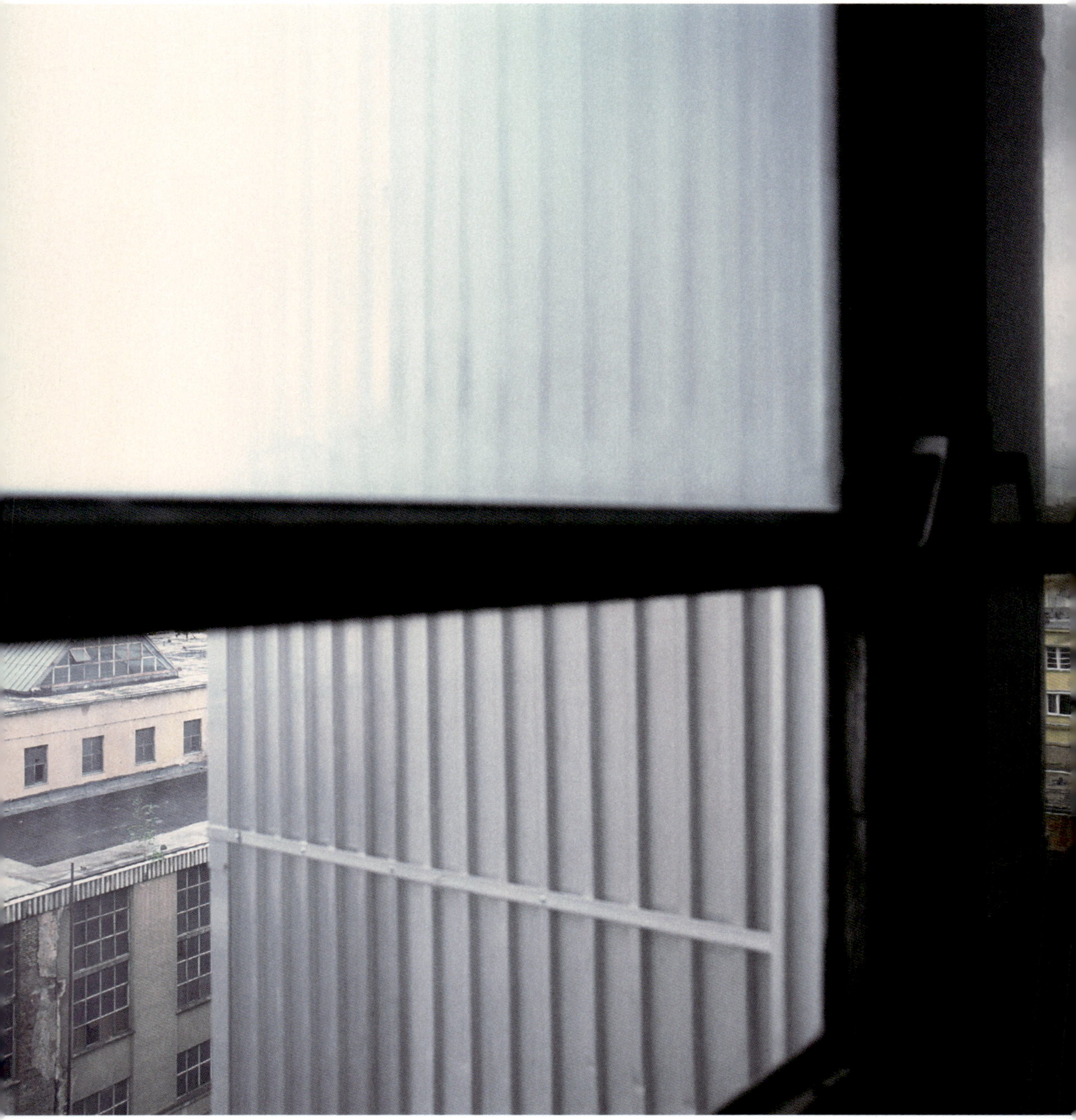

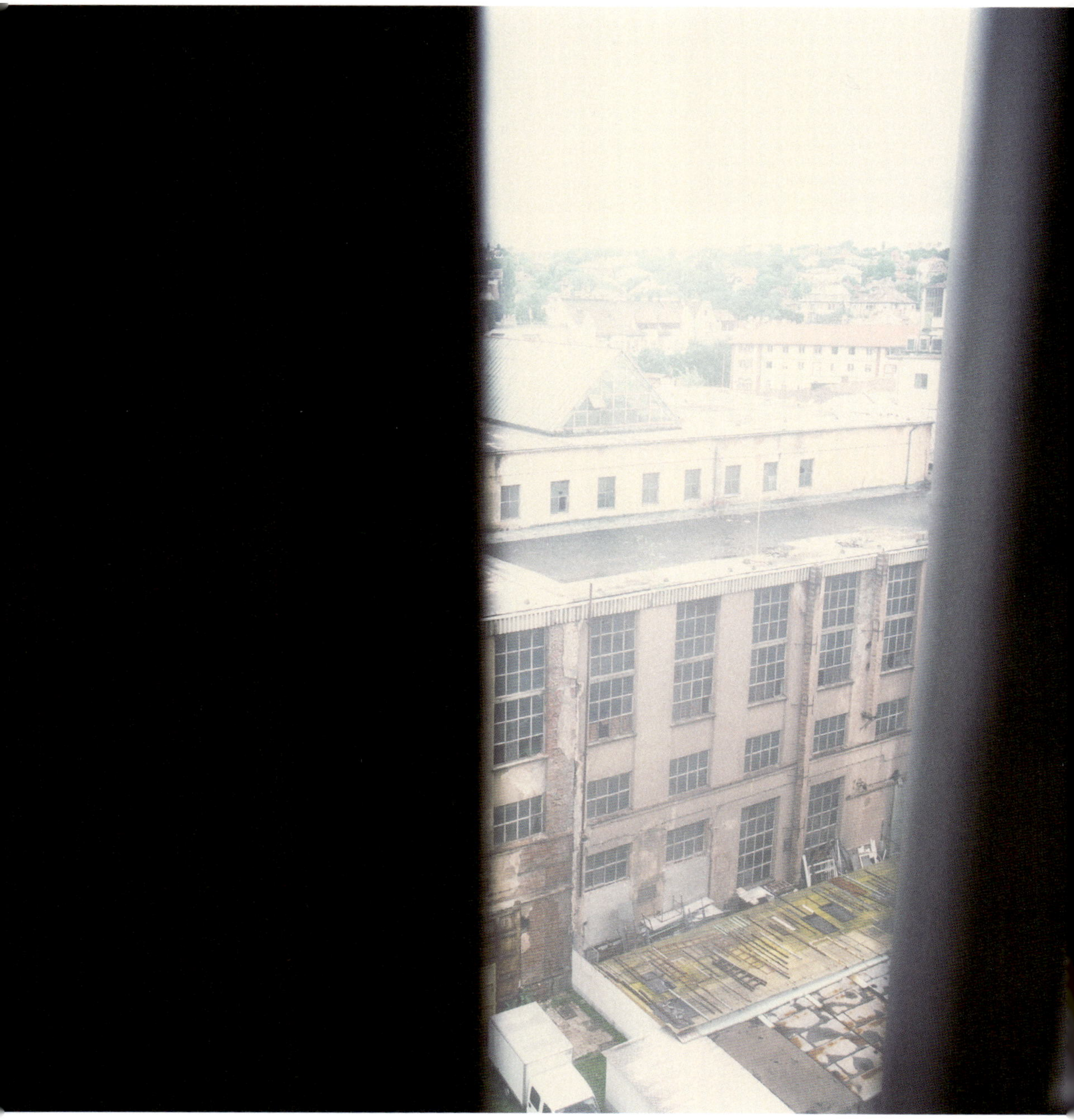

In a South Seas refraction

He had been handed his papers for the job at the steelworks and told to present them at the press department of the Ministry for Production, and without delay moreover, lest the greater part of the remainder of the working day be lost, and in order that Köves might be set immediatly to work at the Ministry, should they see fit. Köves had rushed from one tram to another—the Ministry was near the city centre, a long way from the factory—as if he had been handed some extraordinarily fragile public property: his time, which he had to deliver perfectly intact to its destination, taking care, above all, not even to dream of pilfering any part of it for himself [...].

Ever since arriving in the country, Köves had always had a spot of trouble with time; while living it, it seemed interminable to him, but when he thought about it as the past, it seemed practically nothing, with a duration that might have fitted into a single hour, in all likelihood, the thought crossed Köves's mind, an idle hour at a twilight hour in another, a more real, one might say a more intensive life, somewhere getting on suppertime, when a person has nothing better to do, nor does it matter anyway, and ultimately, it fleetingly occurred to Köves, an entire lifetime was going to pass like that, his life, on which he would eventually be able to look back with the thought that he could have seen to it within the space of a single hour, the rest being a sheer frittering away of time, difficult living conditions, struggle—and all for what?

"All the same…," Sziklai then picked up the thread of their conversation again, "How do you think you got out of the meatgrinder into such a classy job?"

"How?" Köves inquired curiously, but like someone already harbouring forebodings.

"By my organizing it for you," Sziklai wised him up.

"You?!" Köves was astonished. "You mean it wasn't an arrangement from higher up?" He gave himself away, like a child who, driven by his own curiosity, starts taking a doll apart in order to see what is speaking in its belly; and having got going, he also related to Sziklai how he had been dismissed from the steelworks, and Sziklai laughed so hard that a tiny tear welled up in one eye and lodged, twinkling, in the thicket of wrinkles which had formed at the corner of the eye.

"An arrangement from higher up!" he choked. "Well of course it was an arrangement from higher up: I arranged it." He finally calmed down, adding that the press chief was an "old client." […].

"Do you get it now?" Sziklai asked.

"Sure," Köves replied with a thin smile, like someone who admittedly might have been slightly taken in but was nevertheless not entirely oblivious to the funny side of the situation. After which Sziklai once again got Köves to repeat what the head of the shipping department had said, the things about higher conceptualization, unbroken perfectionism, and putting people to the test, the whole situation as they had sat opposite each other and debated things in all seriousness, when he, Sziklai, and the press chief had already talked about and arranged everything ages ago, and having again laughed at the whole thing as if he were hearing it for the first time:

"You see, old chap, now that's a true comic situation for you!"

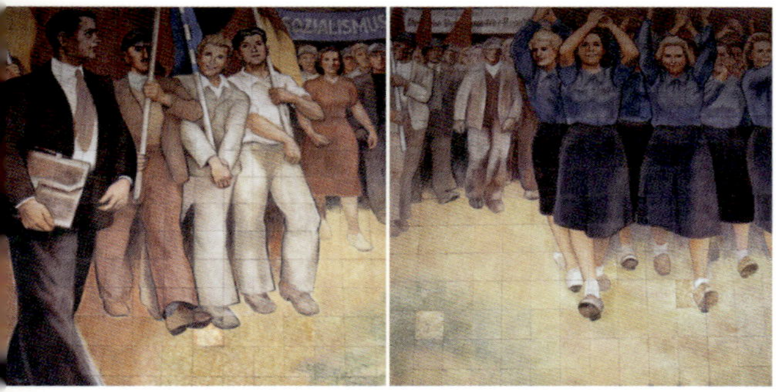
SOZIALISMUS

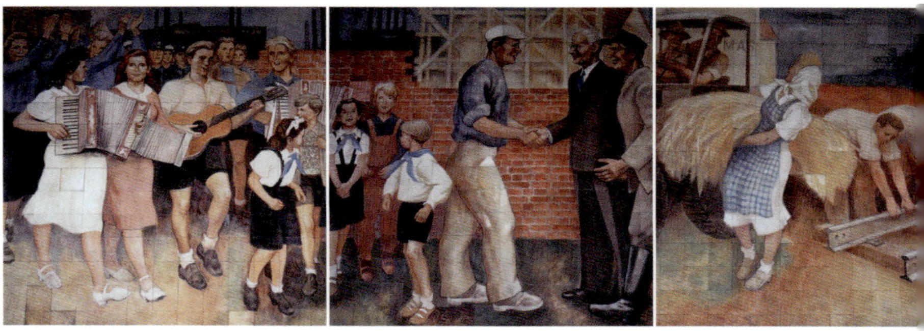

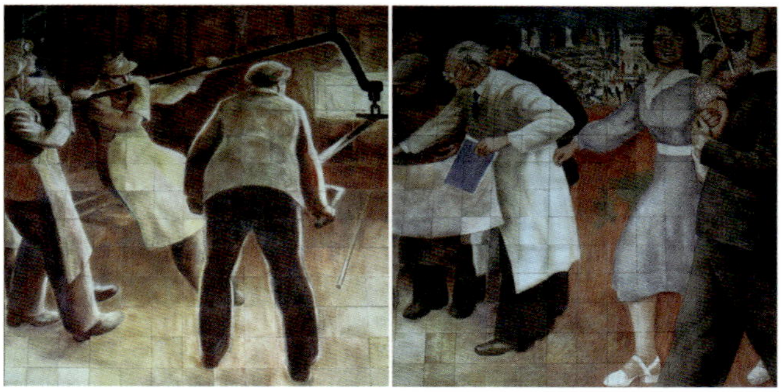

Continuation Köves had better success with literature in the ministry, albeit not in what was strictly his field of work: Köves had no need of any literary talents for his work, though as to what talents were actually needed he never managed to find out. Köves spent his first days at the ministry almost exclusively reading, and more specifically reading the writings of his colleague, the other staffer, or to be more correct (this being his official title): the senior staffer, the press chief, with a somewhat pained smile and now with two flowers in his buttonhole, being of the opinion that these writings would serve Köves as a better introduction into the scope of duties that were awaiting him, and at one and the same time an example to be followed, indeed, he might say—and here the press chief's glance searched out the typist's, as if the two of them knew something to which Köves was not yet privy—he might say, an ideal example.

In the spring of 1951 Imre Kertész got a position in the press department of the *Kohó- és Gépipari Minisztérium* (Ministry for Metallurgy and Mechanical Engineering). Photos: *Aufbau der Republik/ Establishment of the Republic* (1952), mosaic by Max Lingner at the former Ministries Building, which today is the German Federal Ministry for Finance, on the corner of Leipziger Strasse and Wilhelmstrasse, Berlin; pp. 86–87: Stasi Archives Office, former East German Ministry for State Security (MfS) in Berlin-Lichtenberg; p. 93: secretaries with Hungarian television (MTV) and the Ministry for Economics and Transport.

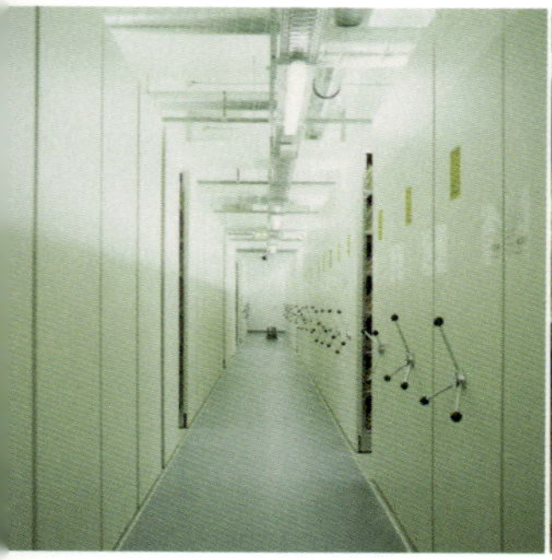
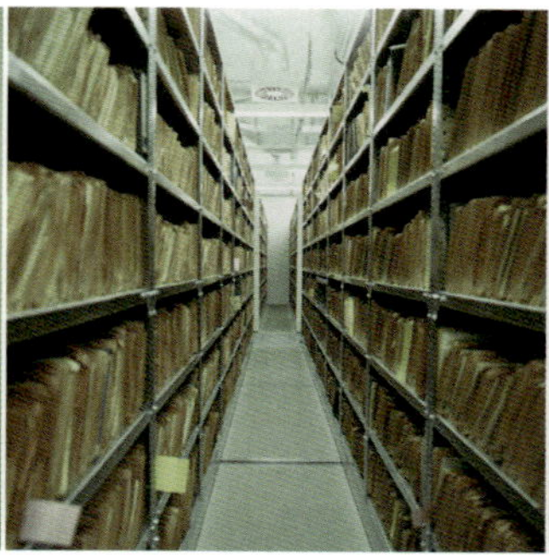
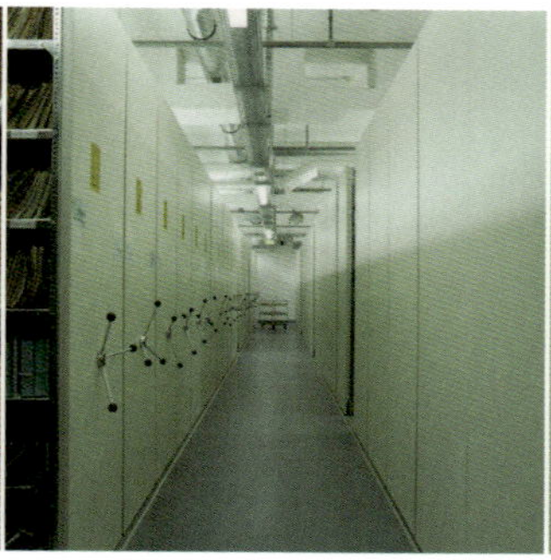
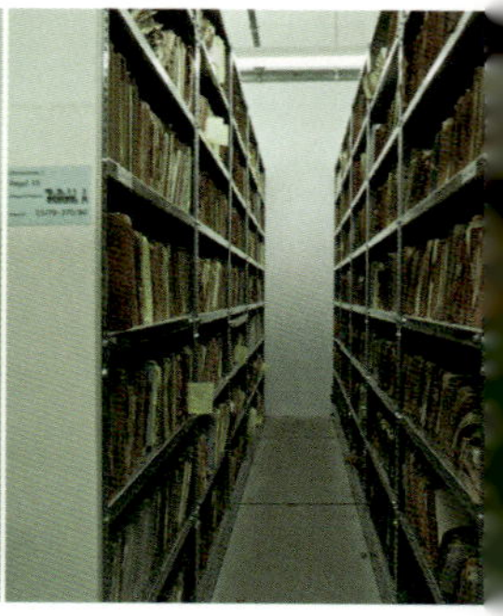
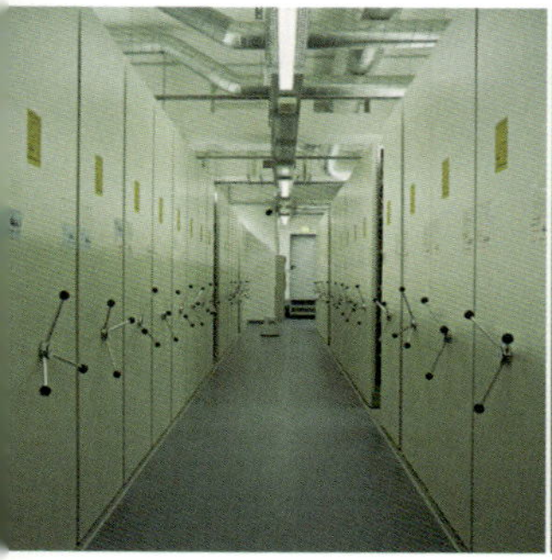
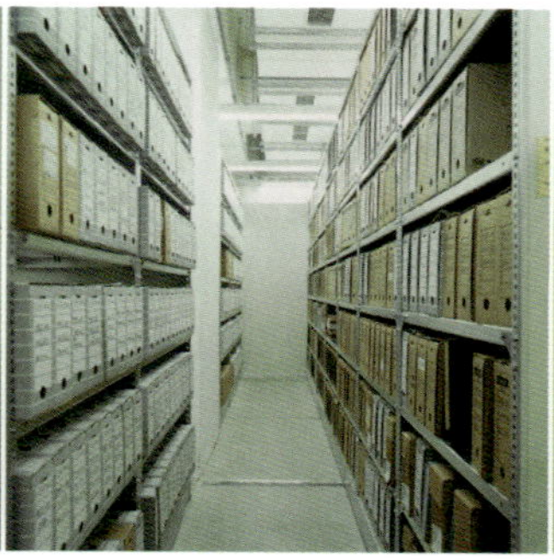
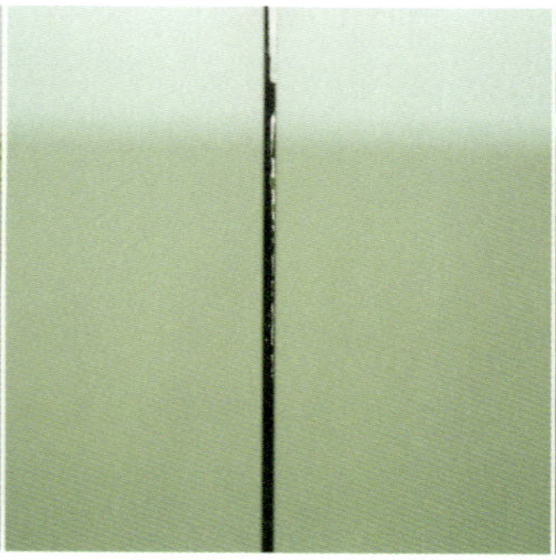
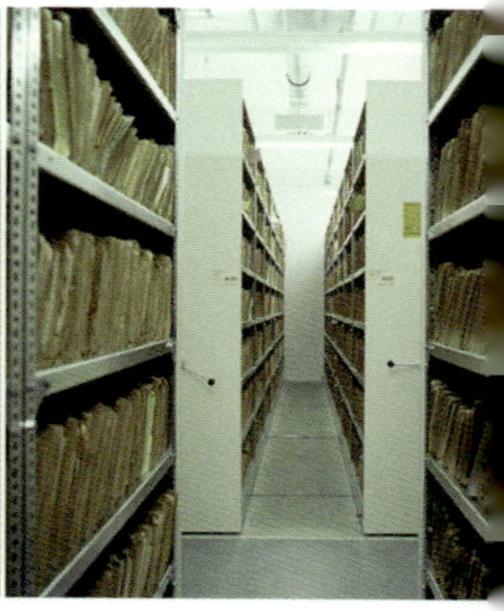

Consequently, Köves lived in a constant torment of uncertainty: almost every day he would produce a piece of writing, longer or shorter, which, as best he could, would be fashioned along the lines set by the senior staffer in respect of its syntax and an outwardly meaningful obscurity, or rather he would keep on amending it until in the end he himself did not understand it, for as long as he was able to understand it even he could see it was meaningless and therefore could not be good, or to be more accurate, could not serve its purpose—a purpose about which Köves was the least clearly aware of all, […].

And when the press chief placed a hand on his shoulder and said to him, albeit in an undeniably amiable tone:

"Would you be so good as to step into my room for a minute?"

Köves got up from his desk like someone who, after much anguish, was almost relieved that he was finally going to hear the sentence passed.

Yet the press chief now leaned back in his chair, adjusted his necktie, then with just a trace of a long-suffering smile and, his head tilted slightly to the side, came out with:

"I'd like to read out a poem to you."

"A poem?" Köves was astonished.

Then, as if to intensify Köves's surprise still further:

"My own," the press chief smiled as he produced a folded sheet of paper from the inside pocket of his jacket, which once again was freshly adorned with a small white-petalled bloom, and slowly—to no little horror on Köves's part—began to unfold it.

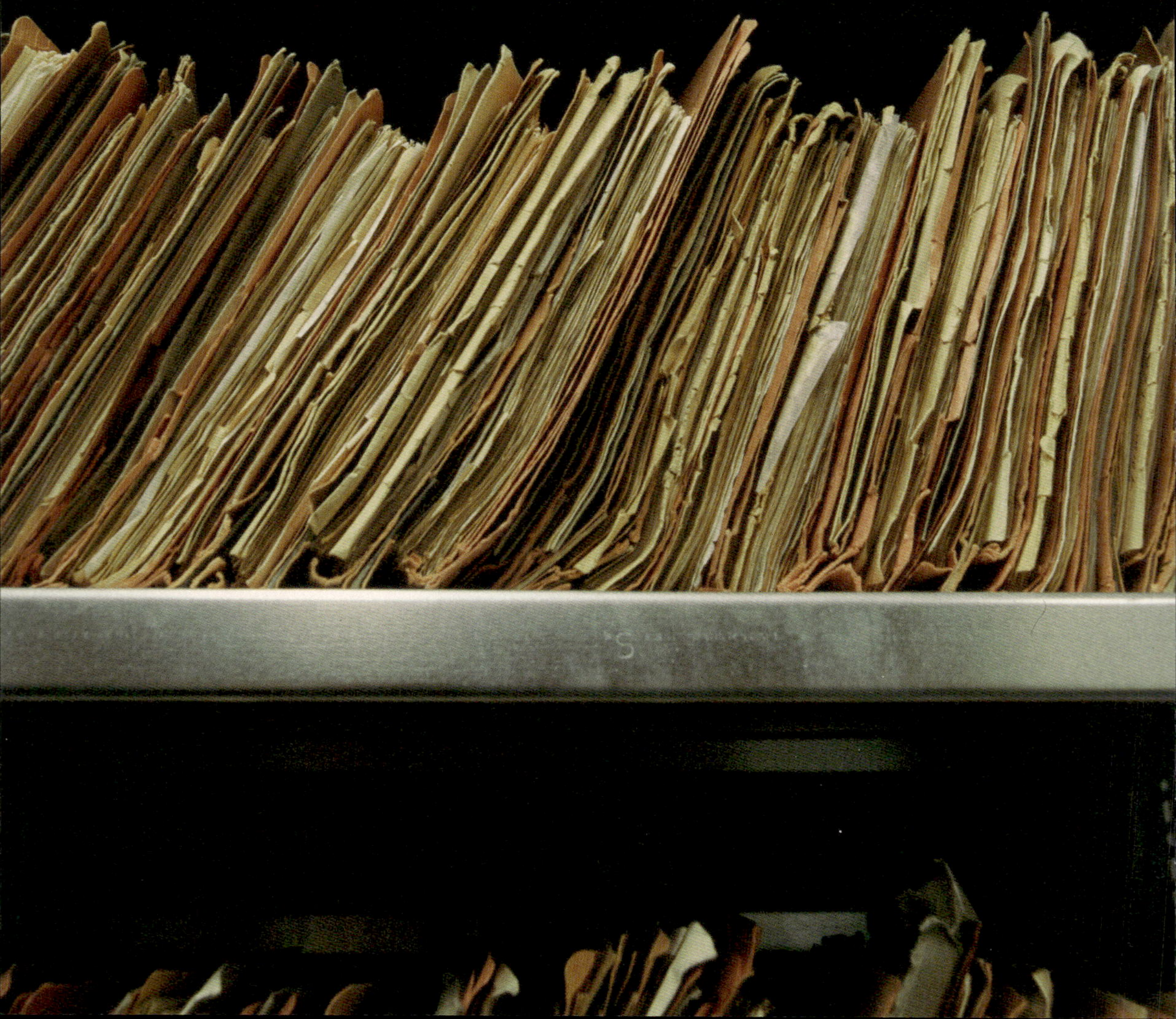

Turning-point. Passion. Back to earth

For notwithstanding the fact that Köves had barely an inkling about poetry (apart from an obviously critical year in his distant childhood, he had never written, or even read, any poems), the press chief seemed to trust in his judgement, because, after the first occasion, he read out his poems to him on a more or less regular basis; […].

He was therefore all the more surprised when, on getting to work that morning, he found the press chief, the senior staffer, and the typist all in the office (they were standing in a group as though they had nothing else to do that day other than, for instance, wait for him), […].

"In that case," the press chief now brought out the hand that up till then he had been hiding behind his back and which was clutching a sheaf of paper, and Köves, if he was not mistaken, was horrified to recognize his own writings, all the many, many assignments he had written and handed over to the press chief since arriving there — "in that case, try to devise some useable communiqués out of this dog's dinner," with which he tossed the entire bundle onto Köves's desk […].

"Poor darling!...," the typist said, or rather whispered in a deep, emotion-laden voice.

"Then let's go to my place, I have a whole apartement," the typist responded in roughly the same tone that Köves had so often heard her using on the telephone on office business.

Once the door had closed behind them, however, they had only just enough time to swiftly get out of their clothes, but not to make the bed as well: they sank onto the gaudy, threadbare carpet, snatching, tumbling about, panting, moaning, as though all they had been doing for centuries, no, millennia, was wait, wait and endure, oppressed and, even under the blows which battered body and soul, concealing within themselves, secretly and as it were slyly, a hope, however preposterous, that their torments would one day, just once, be obliterated by rapture, or if it came to that, that all their torments would one day melt into rapture, from which they would groan just as they had from their torments, for throughout their lives all they had ever learned, ever at all, was to groan.

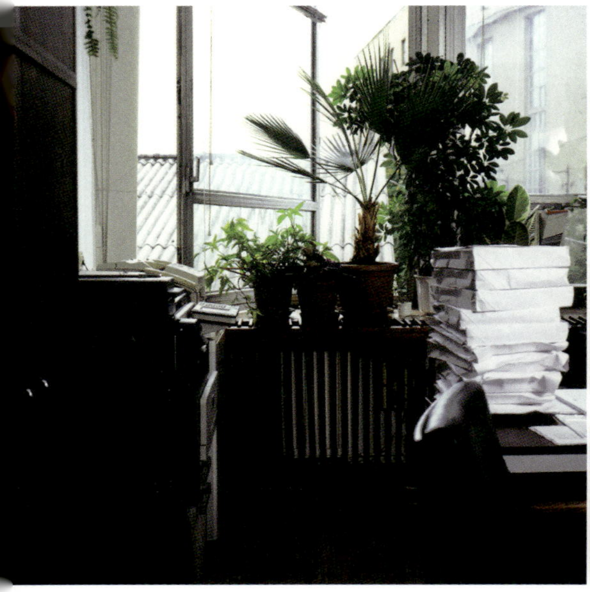
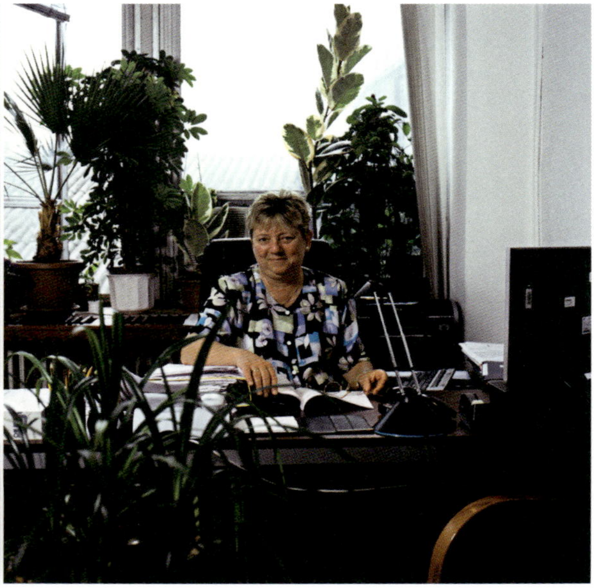
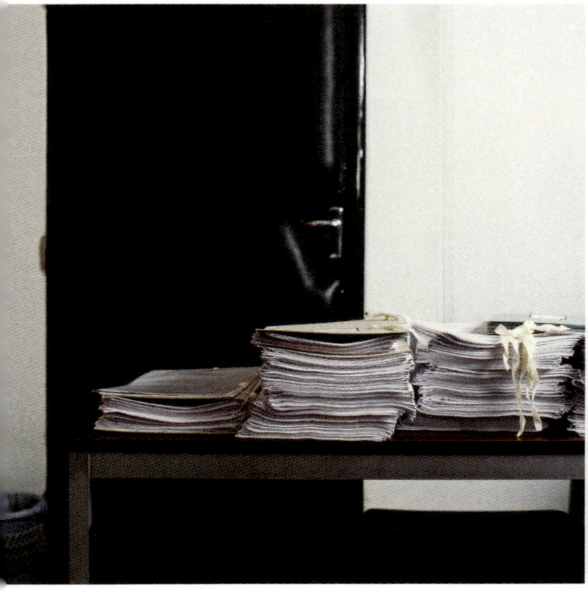
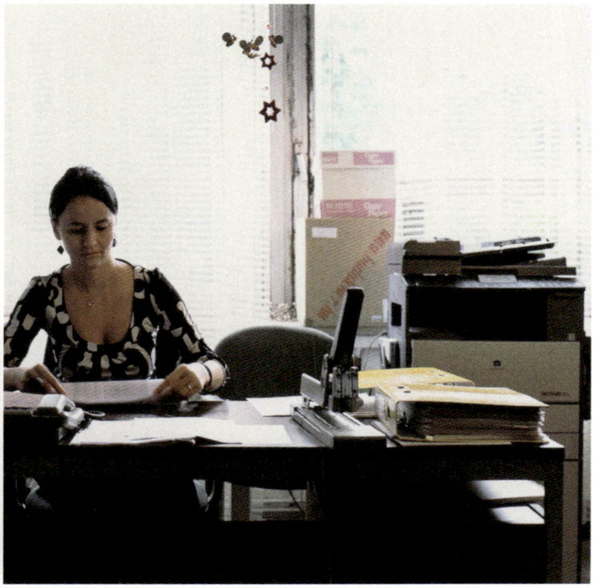

"Did he take you into his confidence? Let you in on his secrets?"

"What secrets?" Köves asked.

"That's his way," the girl said. "First he pours his soul out to you, then he murders you…"

"All he did with me is read out a short story," Köves protested.

In short, it was about the press chief, or rather not the press chief, not a bit of it: the protagonist of the story, a "Wanderer" of some sort (Köves tried to call him to mind) who was roaming around a desert of some kind and all at once arrives at a tower of some kind [...], and in the tower he spies a marvellous woman (come to think of it, it was more than likely the woman's singing which had drawn him to the tower in the first place, it occured to Köves), who now came down to him and led him into her garden, [...].

Anyway, he carried on, while the woman is leading him along these paths, the press chief, or Wanderer (though Köves could only ever imagine the latter amidst the garden scenery in the form of the diminutive, immaculately dressed press chief in some outrageous costume), notices that the woman has heavy shackles on her hands and feet.

The press chief is then overcome by a disagreeable presentiment, except that by now a sense of compassion, to use a mild and by no means accurate word for it, has been awakened in him, and this has stifled more sober considerations, so that he starts to kiss the woman's wounds, and she, in an enigmatic manner, stands up, takes the press chief by the hand, leads him back to the foot of the tower and there, on the moonlit lawn, submits to his passion.

Because a horrifying cry resounds, and a strapping, sinister man in black appears in the doorway to the tower, a cat-o'-nine-tails in his hand—the man of the house and the woman's husband, who in all probability has seen everything from one of the tower's windows.

The man of the house "sets his servants and hounds loose" on the press chief. The woman pleads for mercy, first for the two of them but, as the man raises the lash on her, forgetting the press chief, for herself alone, at which the man pulls the woman up and clasps her to his chest. The press chief, who in the meantime has been struggling with "the servants and hounds," now catches the woman's glance, reading compassion from it and something else: "stolen rapture." His strength then fails him, and he yields to "the servants and hounds." He possibly even dies, or at least the woman and the man suppose so. Nevertheless, he can still see and hear.

The sinister couple now sink to the ground and try to make love on the lawn, glimmering in the silver of the moonlight, right next to the press chief's corpse. The man might have triumphed, but to no avail; the woman tries out in vain all the tricks and secrets of love that she has just learned from the press chief, so in the end they clamber to their feet on the turf and stand there, broken and overwhelmed with shame, tears glistening in their eyes. "Not even now?...," the woman asks gently.

"Not even now," the man replies, his head lowered.

[…] In the meantime he has somehow pulled himself together and, evading the vigilance of servants and hounds, made good his escape, and with his "lacerated wounds" he is now moving around outside anew, in the desert maybe, but free at last.

"Free!" the typist's unexpected, unduly shrill exclamation brought Köves round, almost making him jump. "The wretch!…He'll never be free," she added bitterly […].

"Do you really know nothing?" the typist asked, and it really did seem that Köves knew nothing, nothing at all. "The current chairman of the Supervisory Committee!…The bitch!"

"She is permanently the current chairman of the Supervisory Committee; by pure chance she is always the current one, her, her, and no-one else, it's been going on like that for years, and it will go on like that for still more years!…Who is going to dare stand up to her husband?"

"Why? Who's that?" Köves asked, more due to the pause that ensued, which seemed to be demanding his voice, confirmation of his presence, rather than out of any genuine curiosity.

"The minister's secretary," the girl retorted with the same bitterness as before, though this time it carried a near-exultant ring of delight at being well informed.

"You mean there's a minister?" Köves marvelled, […].

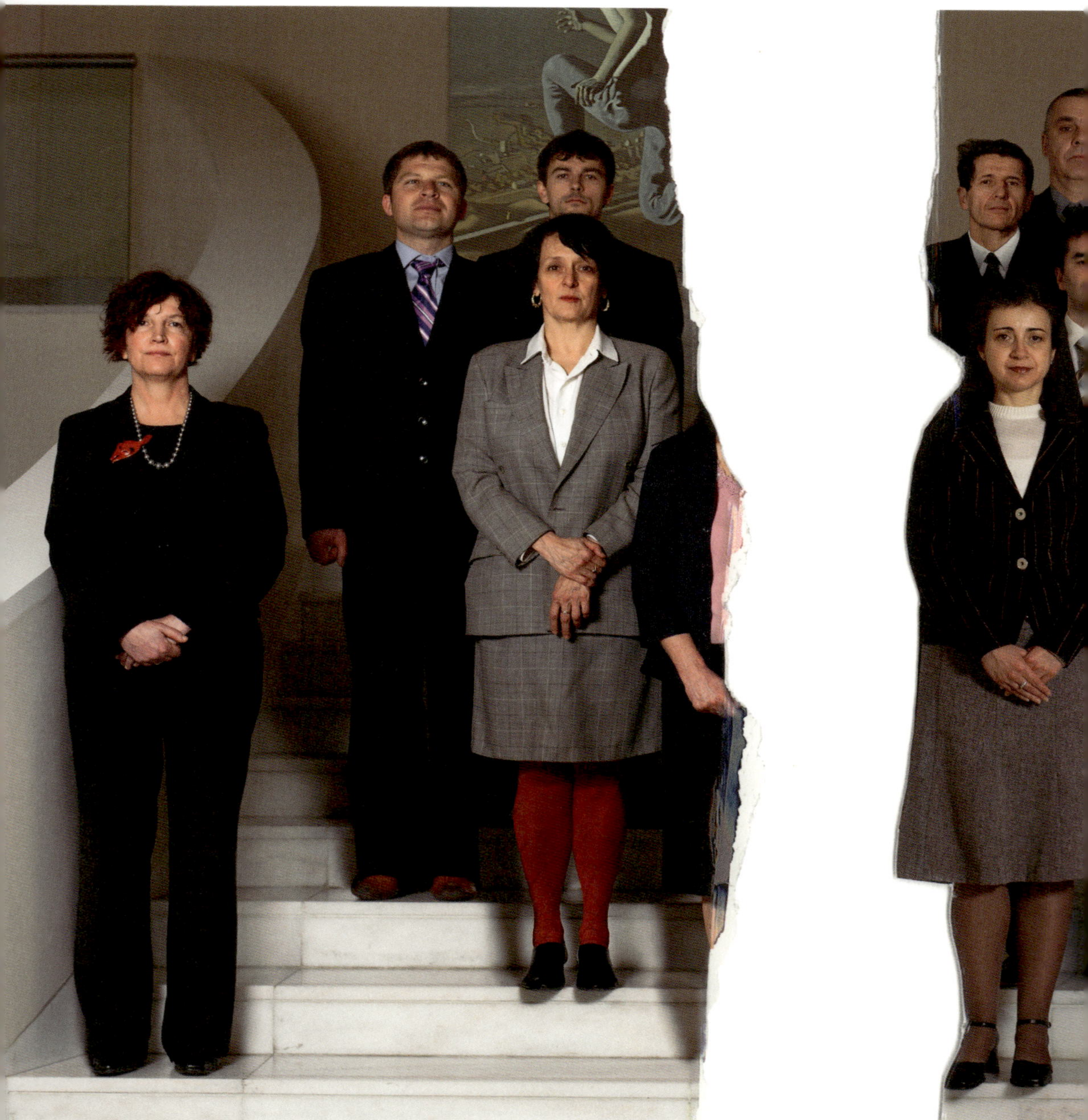

Inspired by the manipulated photographs from the Stalist era, the photographic construction of a group portrait was created by means of analogue (pp. 100–101) and digital (pp. 102–103) retouching. In the background on pp. 102–103, *Die Flucht des Sisyphos/The Flight of Sisyphus* (1972) by Wolfgang Mattheuer was added to the image.

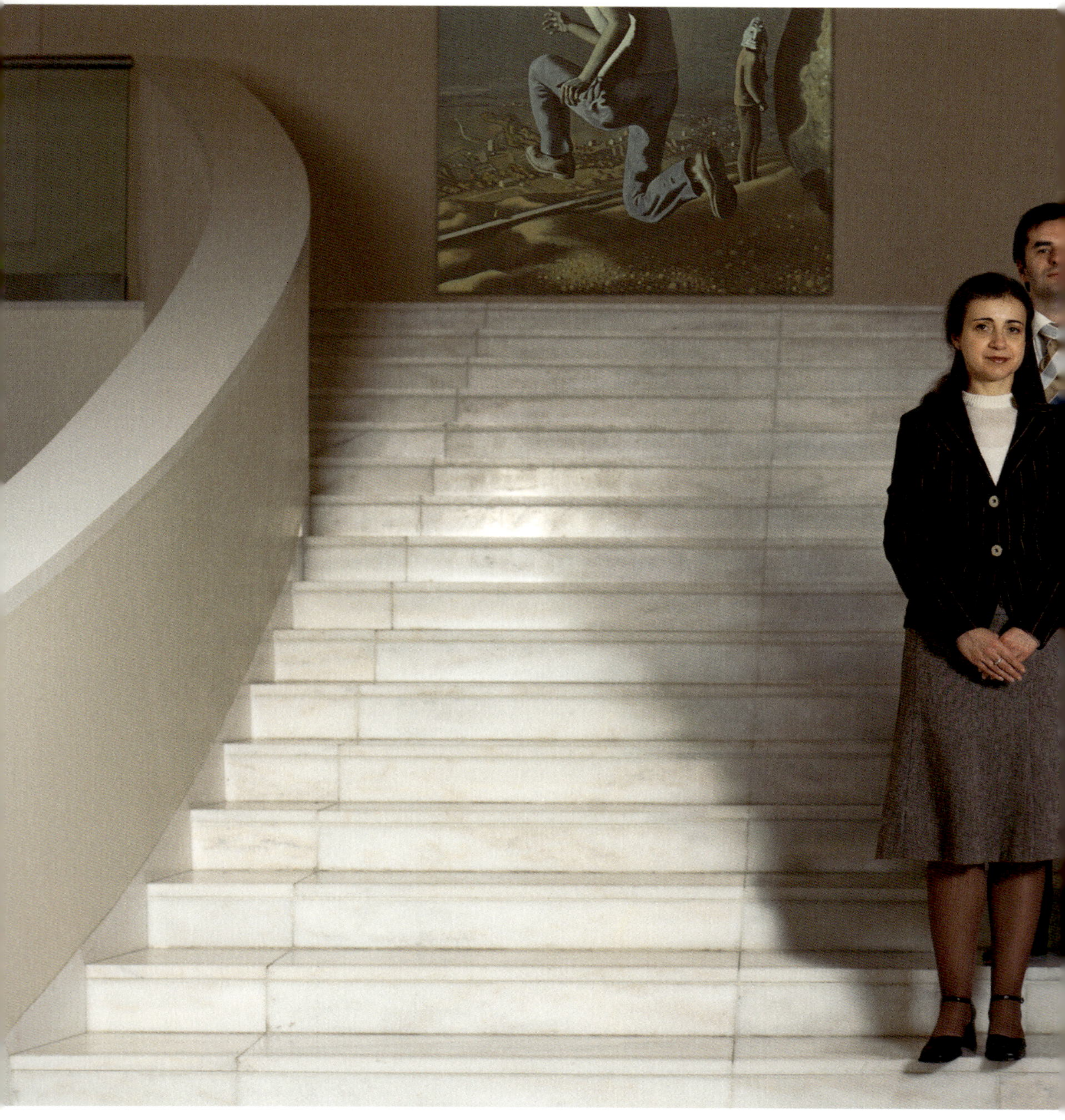

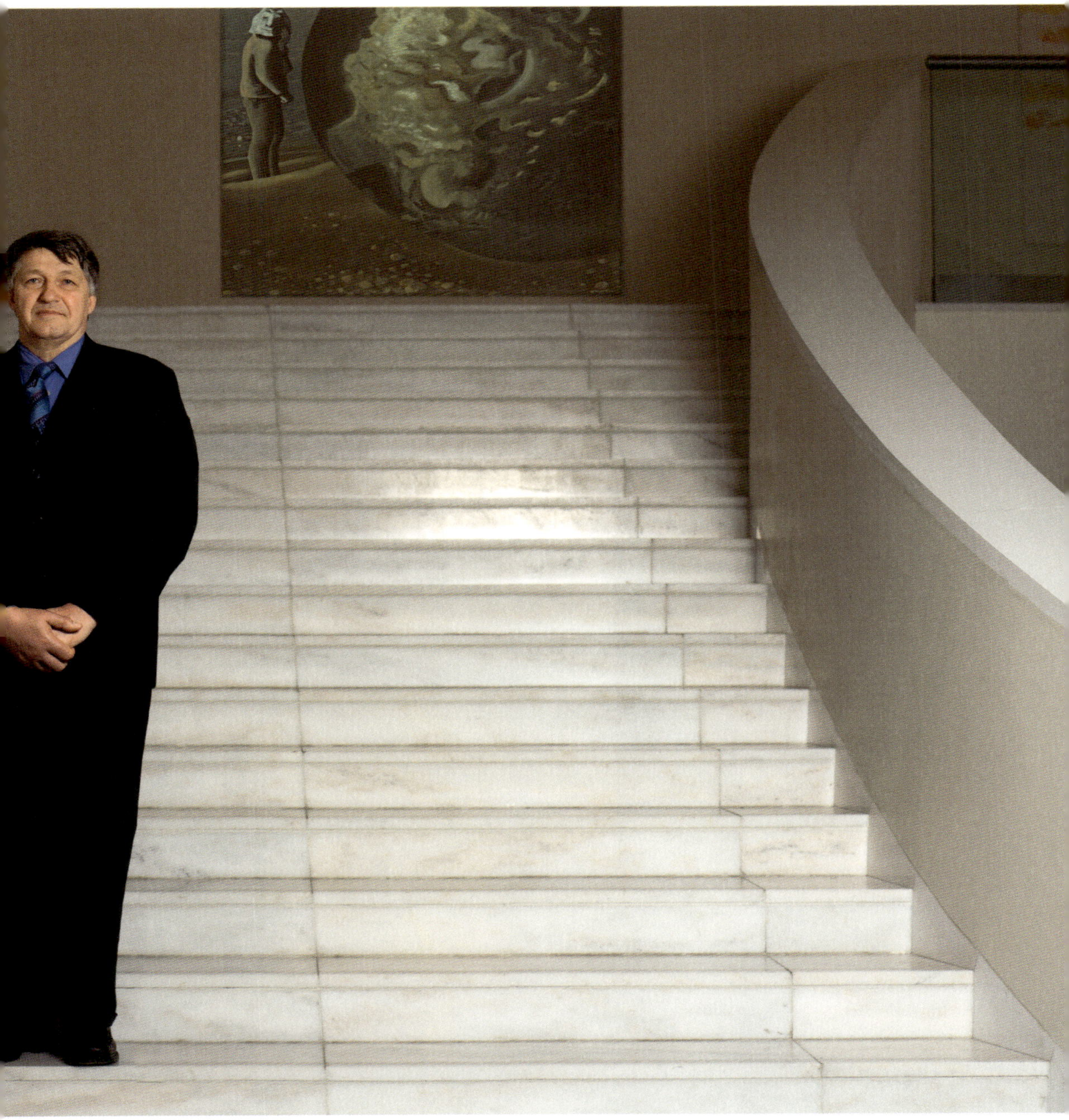

The minister—he existed all right, he was all too real! And even more real was his power, power in general. A ramifying thread which interwove everything and twitched everyone to do its bidding. There might be some individuals whom he did not reach, or who even did not see him—Köves for one, who therefore did not have the foggiest idea about him. [...] It was valid to ask, of course, whether it was possible to live like that, at least over a protracted period—outside the circle, that is.

Köves was not even aware, the girl continued, that his situation... and here she hesitated as if she were trying to find the appropriate words with which to alert Köves to his situation: his situation was the most precarious, the most fragile, in the department, he being the only person who was completely dispensable.

Yet when he tried to approach her: "Don't touch me!" the girl exclaimed, then "Get going, go!" she added in a sudden fit of anger that Köves felt he did not deserve as he had done nothing to upset the girl, or if he had, then it was not deliberate: "Just so you don't get the idea that I'm going to walk arm in arm with you to the ministry where your notice of dismissal is waiting!"

"Notice of dismissal?" Köves was astonished, not so much at the news in itself, more at its unexpectedness, startled solely by the setting, the timing, and the occasion. "How do you know?" he asked a little later, and of course he had not the slightest intention of setting off.

"I typed it yesterday morning."

Change of direction "You're writing?…," Köves asked after a short lull, quietly and, involuntarily, with a degree of sympathetic tact.

Berg, spreading his arms a little and grimacing, made the irritated admission:

"Yes, I'm writing," like someone who had been caught in a shameful passion that he himself deprecated.

"And what?" Köves probed further, after allowing another considerate pause to go by, to which Berg, in wonder, raised a glance, as it were, looking past Köves:

"What?…" the question came back, as if this were the first time he had thought about it. "The writing," he then declared […].

"What's the writing about?"

"Mercy," Berg responded promptly, without a moment's hesitation.

"I see," said Köves, although he couldn't really have seen as he followed it straightaway by asking: "And what do you mean by 'mercy'?"

"The necessary," came the answer, as swiftly as before.

"And what is necessary?" Köves plugged away, as though sensing that the moment was favourable and wishing to make use of it […].

Berg then seemed to be struggling but in the end only took a sip of water, then, without taking any notice of Köves, articulating clearly in his sonorous voice, began reading very clearly, starting with the title, which in itself was slightly disconcerting, even startling:

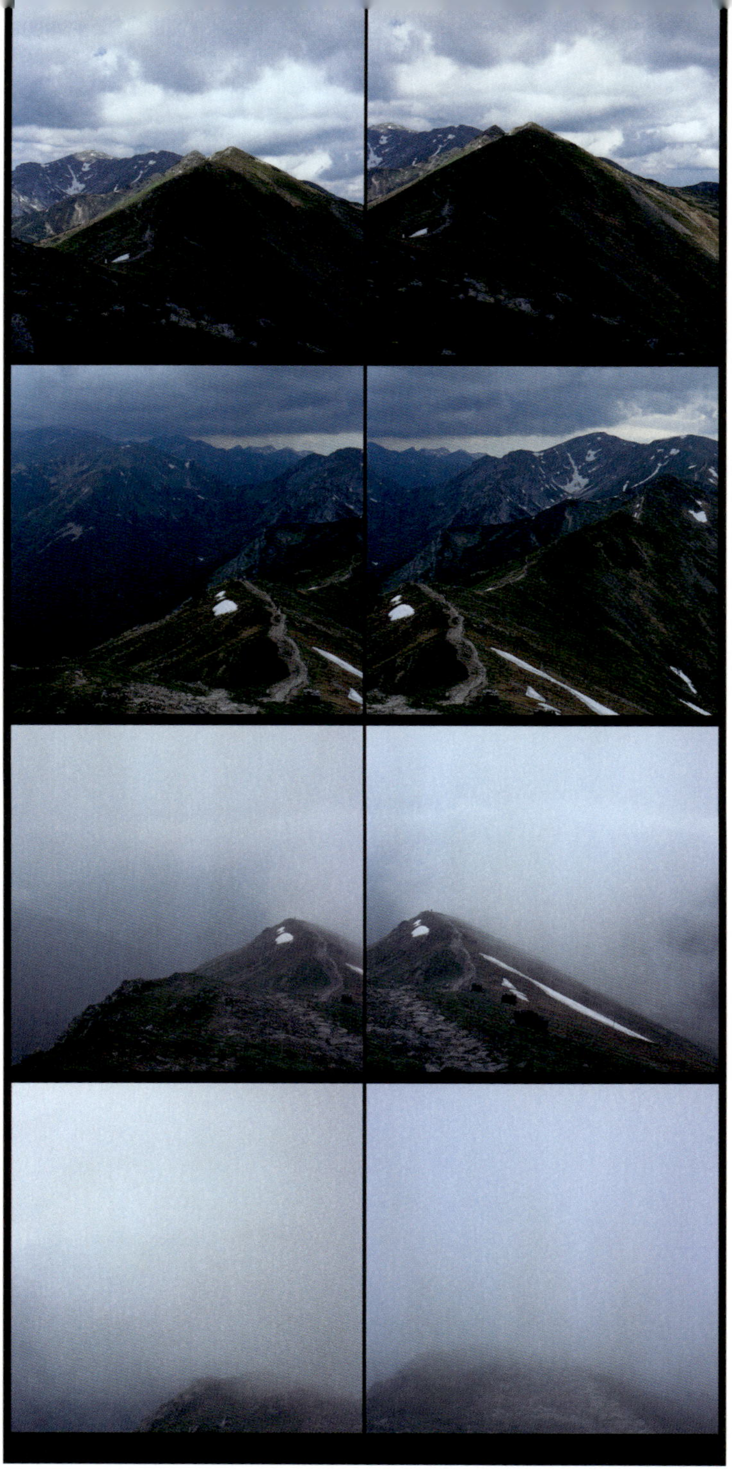

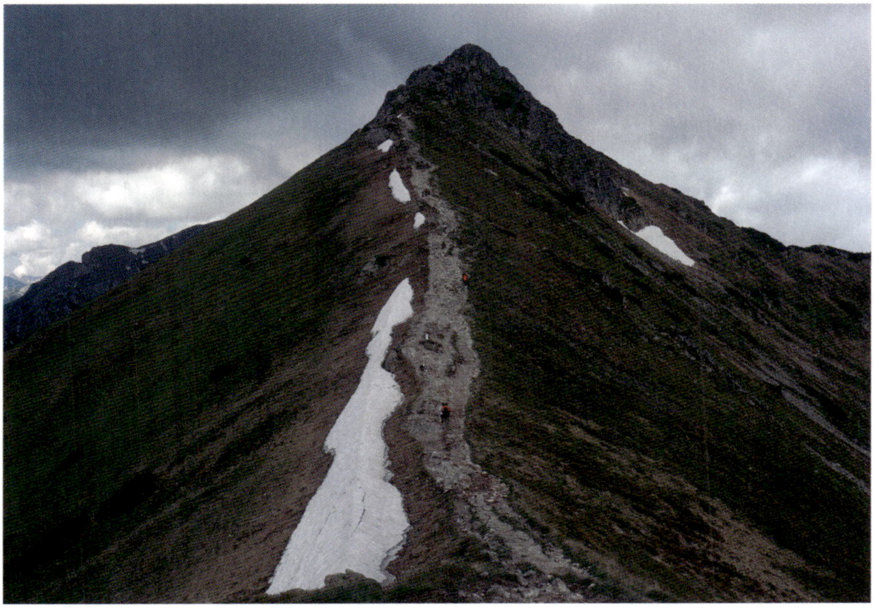

"**I, the executioner…** *I, who will stand before the court accused of causing the deaths of 30,000 people, am able to transcend my fate, and to my pleasant surprise — obviously to the world's surprise as well — I still feel that much responsible interest toward life as not to be ashamed of spending my last days and hours with moralising — rather appropriately and not unskilfully, you have to admit.*

[...] You would most happily see me as some kind of savage, a strange wild animal; in any case as a person who is utterly foreign to your nature; with whom you can have nothing at all to do at the level of living contacts, and you derive satisfaction from the fact that the false reality created by my acts serves such assumptions perfectly, because you are not in the least curious about the fuller reality—I understand that endeavour, yet I still make so bold as to furnish the information that it is nothing more than self-delusion, which is not worthy of you. And now that I am modestly but categorically declaring my right to my human condition, my relevance to the general, you wish to have nothing to do with me; you avert your gazes from me in the name of morality lest I impel you to even the slightest bit of understanding or sympathy for me—that is to say, lest in me you should recognize yourselves to even the slightest degree.

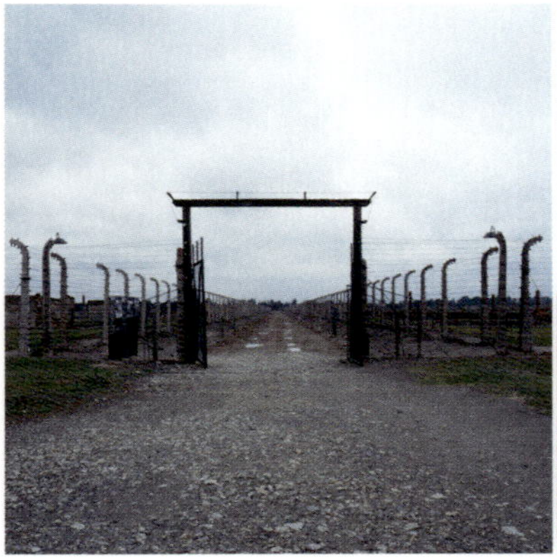
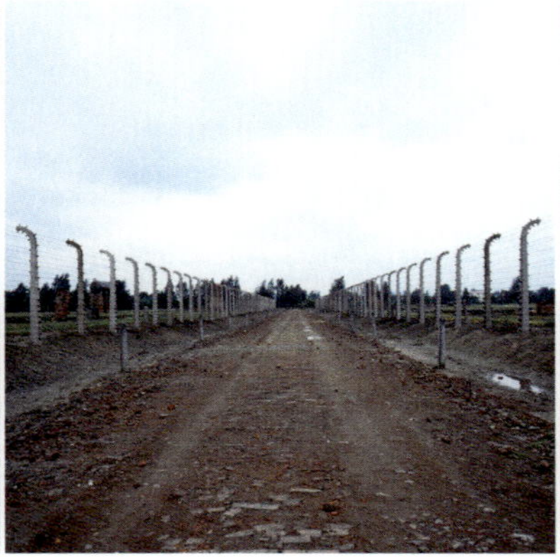
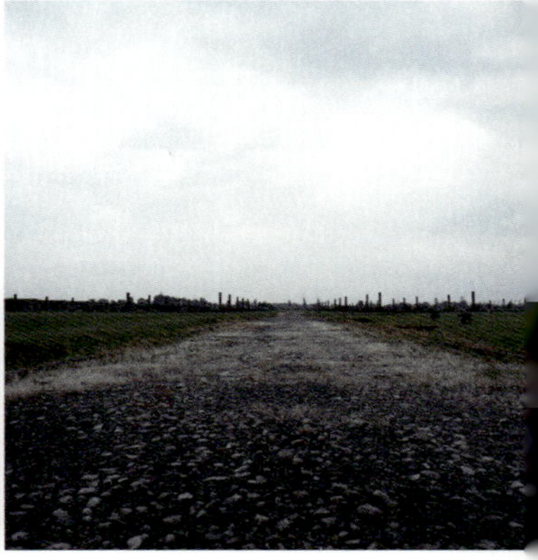
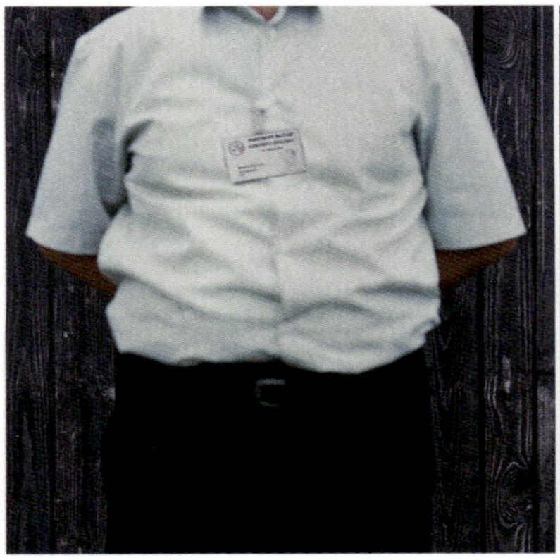
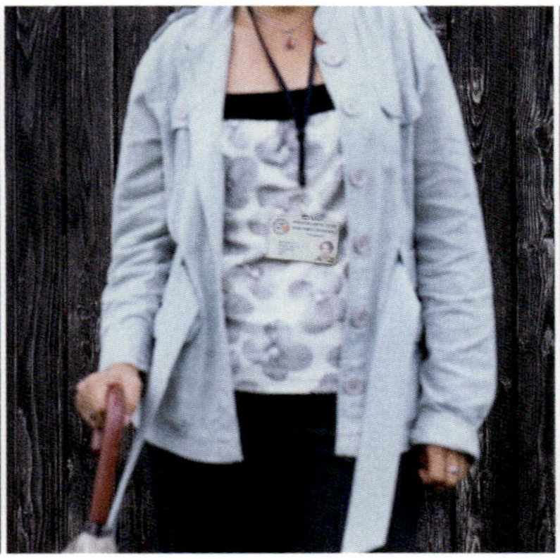
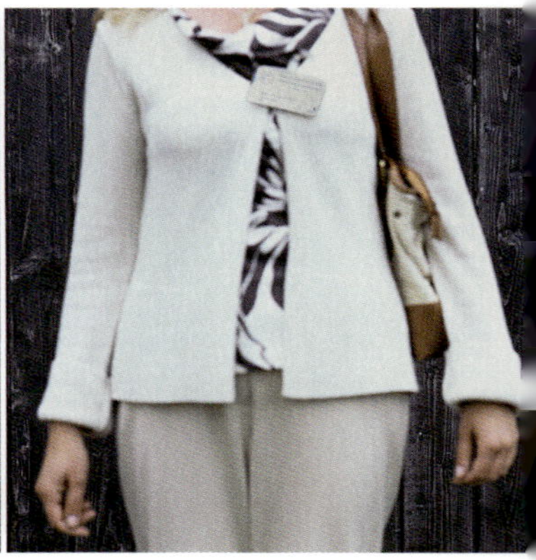

111

So, what was it that I wanted to say? Nothing other than that you should recognize your salvation in my excessively wild fate, inasmuch as it might have been your fate, and inasmuch as I lived it, not despite, but instead of you.

Yes, when I committed my definitive act—the first act of murder, which subsequently proved to be an irrevocable choice, just because it had happened, and because it could have happened—that is, the opportunity was presented to do it, and in point of fact an opportunity was not presented to do anything else—so when, under pressure of external compulsion, I committed my definitive act, that pressure of external force, as you will see in the course of the ensuing plot, was not present at all—it did no more than simply accumulate within me, became an inner compulsion, which is to say that it returned to its original form.

And the loose strands of an external compulsion which were not the bonds of a genuine will could easily be torn asunder by the world. But no, the world did nothing; it awaited events with bated breath; it wanted to see what would happen, only then to be horrified by it — horrified by itself.

If you are inclined to look more deeply into yourselves, you will understand me. Because, Ladies and Gentlemen, we have been hopelessly locked up together with one another in this world in miserable camaraderie; everything which happens carries such significance that we can no longer disperse it, nullify it, deny it from each other.

Grounds, objections and a sad final conclusion

"That's it," he smiled. "What do you mean?!" Köves spluttered. "You didn't even get started!"

"To be precise, you heard the preface," Berg informed him. "That's as far as I have got. The rest has yet to come."

"At least give me an idea what happens over the course of the plot," Köves grumbled. "Who is that fellow, anyway? Who did you take by way of example?"

"Who would I take it from if he were foreign to me?" Berg responded to the question with a question.

"You mean to say," Köves was incredulous, "you are that fellow?"

"Let's just say that's one of the possibilities," Berg replied. "One possible path to grace."

"And what other paths might be possible?" Köves wanted to know.

"That of the victim," came the answer.

"And writing?" Köves piped up again. "Isn't writing grace?"

"No," Berg's high voice snapped back as a curt yelp.

"Well what, then?"

"Deferment. Ducking. Dodging," Berg itemized. "The postponement—impossible of course—of the election of grace."

"In other words," Köves asked, "you are either executioner or victim?"

"Both," Berg answered in a slightly impatient tone, like someone who is required to provide information on matters that have long been known.

"What is that...," he began a question with a pensive look on his face, "that definitive first act that, if I rightly recall, the hero commits under pressure of external compulsion, yet nevertheless without the external force being present at the time?"

"Yes," Berg started as though bringing his mind back from dwelling on other things, "that's a decisive, I might almost say crystal-clear passage in the construction. Still, what the act is I don't exactly know as yet — it's something I still have to work out," he said, and brushed it aside.

"In that case," Köves was curious, "how does he know that he's going to commit it?"

"He has to commit it, because, as I say, the construction is ready to hand." Berg was growing impatient. "The opening and the end for sure; it's just the path stretching between that I don't yet see quite clearly."

"Yes," Köves said, "and that path is life itself."

The rock successions were formed in the Polish Tatra (the outer Eastern Carpathians), the mountains between Budapest and Auschwitz. For his literary ego, Imre Kertész took as his model the stone-rolling Sisyphus-as-a-happy-person in the sense of the Camus character. "True, Sisyphus (and labour service) is timeless, but his stone is not immortal. On its bumpy path, through being rolled so many times, in the end it wears down and, all of a sudden, it occurs to Sisyphus that for a long, long time, whistling to himself as he is lost in thought, he has been been kicking a grey lump of stone before him in the dust." (p. 361)

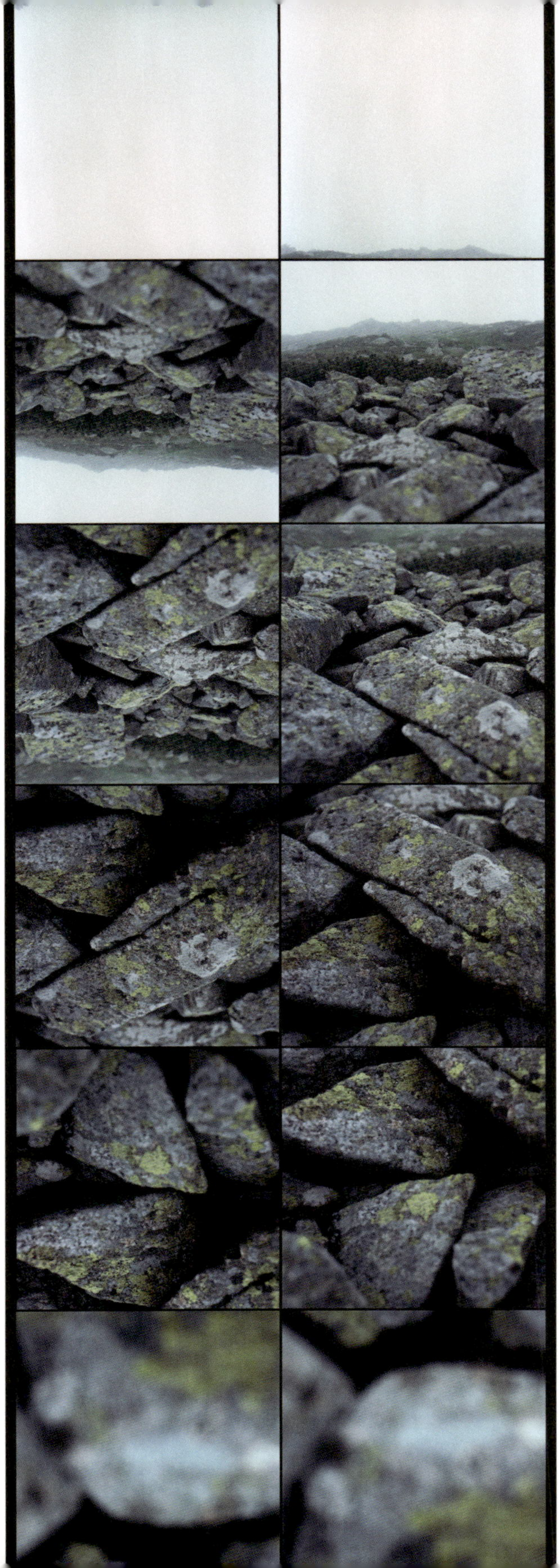

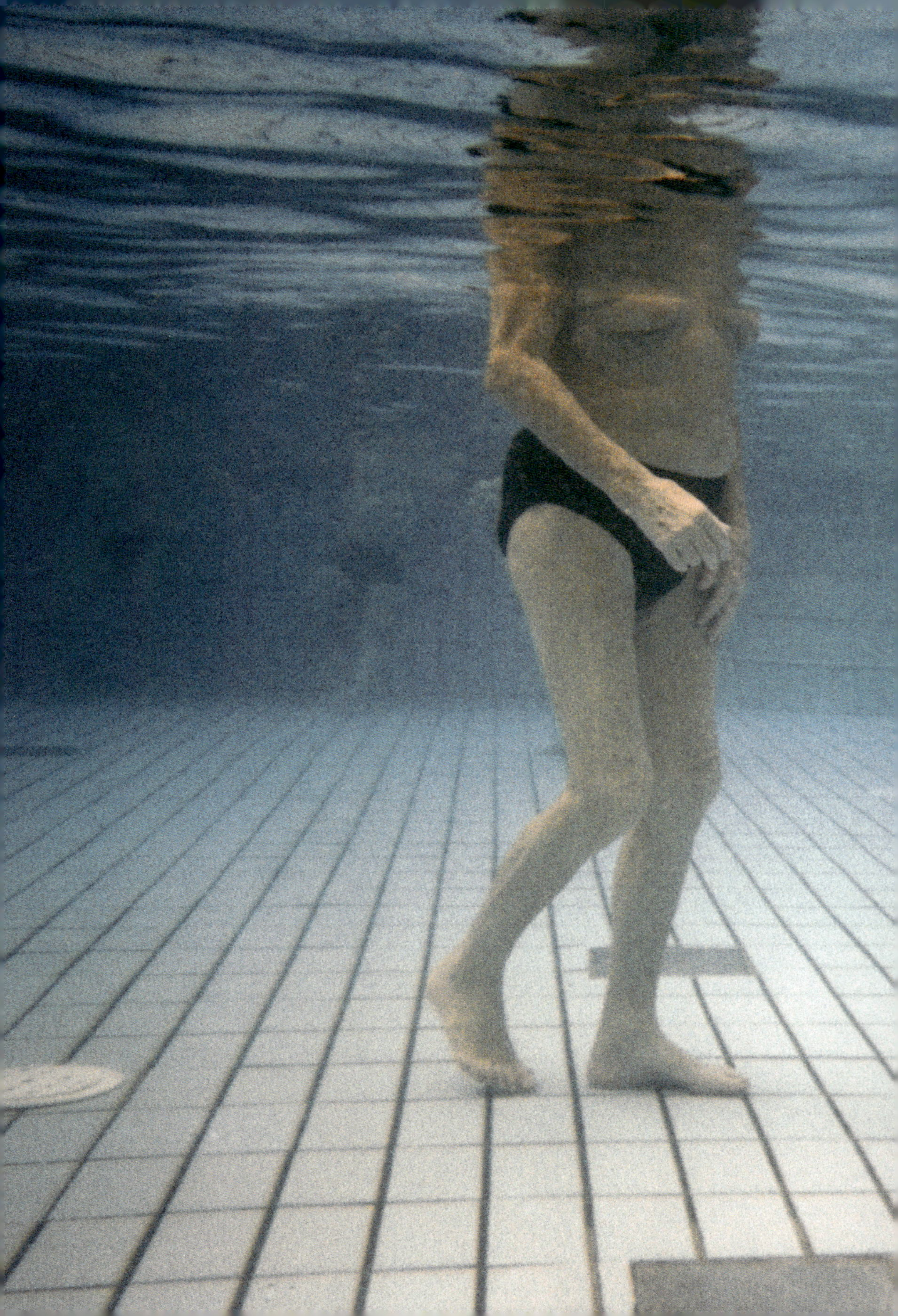

**Köves returns.
     Changes.
The drowing man**

One fine day, Köves turned up again at the South Seas; he had not been there for a long time, he had been in the army, because the same post as the dismissal letter from the ministry had also brought a demand that he immediatly discharge his deferred military service, at which the army had sniffed him in and swallowed him up, until the day came when even it could stomach him no longer and one morning—it happened to be during the solemn moments when general orders are read out—he dropped full length on the floor, almost knocking over a chair and two fellow squaddies in the process, then showed no inclination to return to his senses, despite being disciplined, punished, taken to task, and pilloried, so he was finally carted off to hospital, where he was surrounded by suspicious doctors who cross-questioned him, took samples of his blood, tapped his limbs, thrust a needle into his spine, and—just at the point when he was fearing he would be unmasked, with the attendant, none too promising consequences—abruptly and most unceremoniously, so he barely had time even to be surprised, though there was plenty of reason for that, he was discharged, because one of the checks had shown that one of his thighs was an inch thinner than the other and, even though Köves was unaware of it, he was probably suffering from muscular dystrophy. Sziklai's face split into a thousand pieces from laughter when Köves told him the whole story:

"They could hardly wait to get rid of you, old chap!" he slapped Köves on the thigh in question and put the fortunate outcome of the affair "solely down to the changes."

"What changes?" Köves was amazed, being up to date on nothing since he had been recently preoccupied with rather different matters.

Yet Sziklai did not appear to be much better informed than him:

"Can anyone know?!" he almost reproached Köves for his tactlessness, and it had been so long since Köves had heard the question that, for the first time since he had been discharged from hospital and the army, he was almost seized by a feeling of having found his way back home.

"In any event, one can sense winds of change," Sziklai went on, […].

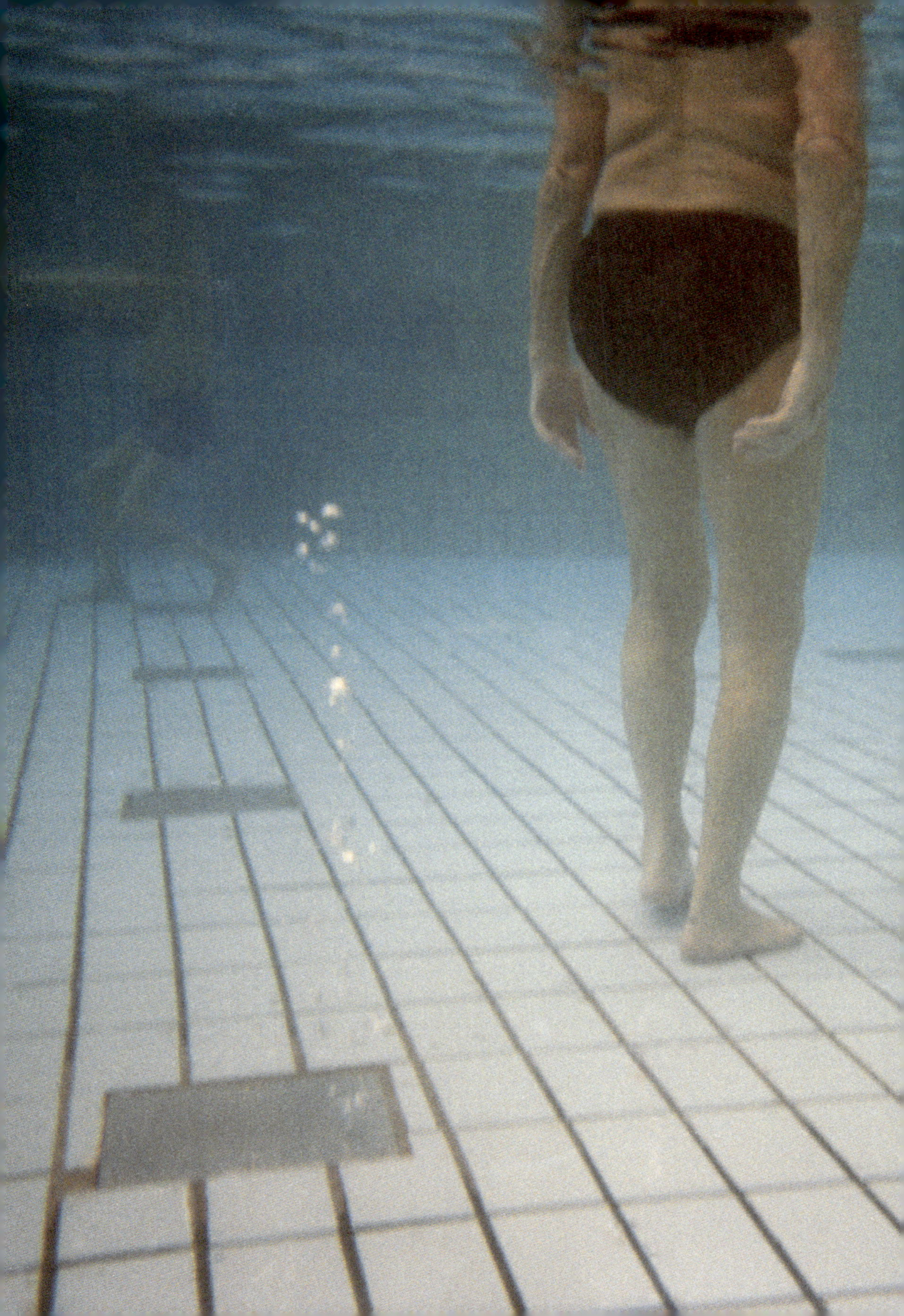

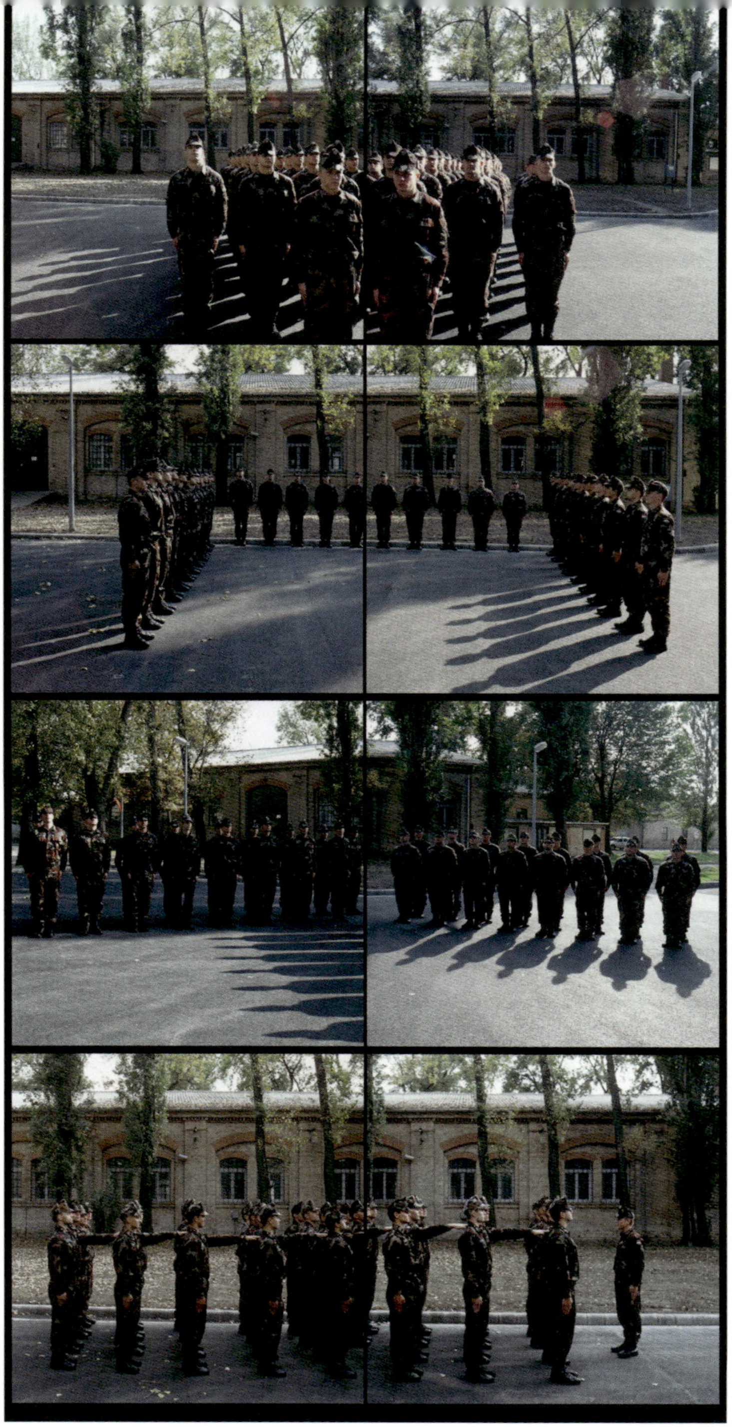

Letter. Consternation   *In short, I want to be of assistance to you, because you can't deny that you are stuck. I believe you when you say that "the construction is ready to hand," but there is something looming up between the "man of intellect and culture" and 30,000 corpses—maybe it too is just a corpse, but in any event the first, and thus the most important, because the question is whether it can be stepped over or ultimately presents an insurmountable barrier. Yes, that definitive first act which subsequently "proves to be an irrevocable choice," if I rightly recall, just because it happened, and because it could have happened, [...].*

So listen!
Let's start with me being called up by the army. I was reluctant to comply with the call-up order, in the way one is always reluctant to fulfil one's personal destiny, all the more so as one usually does not perceive it as such.

It's not true that one's personality ceases to exist; it's more that it is multiplied, which is not a big difference, of course.

In 1951 Imre Kertész was called up for military service. After basic training, his unit was deployed as a guard for the military prosecutors to take accused prisoners to and from prison or their workplaces. Kertész pretended he was having a nervous breakdown, got admitted to hospital and went from there to the army's film institute. Photos: Cadets in their second year of training in various formations on the grounds of the *Zrínyi Miklós Nemzetvédelmi Egyetem* (University for National Defence); pp. 127–132: Guards and cells in the *Márianoszta* prison.

The barracks town was situated in some unknown part of the country, on a desolate plain, where the wind whistled incessantly and bells from the distant settlements tolled incessantly, and I well remember one dawn, when I was standing in line in the open air, in front of the kitchen, holding a mug for coffee: the sun had just risen, the sky was hanging dirtily and shabbily above us; my underpants (in which, just beforehand, I had been performing physical jerks to orders that had been barked out through megaphones) were clinging, clammy from rain and sweat, to my skin when, all of a sudden — through an indefinable decaying stench, compounded of ersatz coffee, soaked clothes, sweaty bodies, fields at daybreak, and latrines — broke a memory, though it was as if the memory was not mine, but somebody else's whom I seemed to remember having seen once in a similar situation, some time long ago, somewhere else, a long way away, in a sunken world lying far beyond the chasms of all prohibitions, dimly and by now barely discernibly, a child, a boy who was once taken away to be murdered.

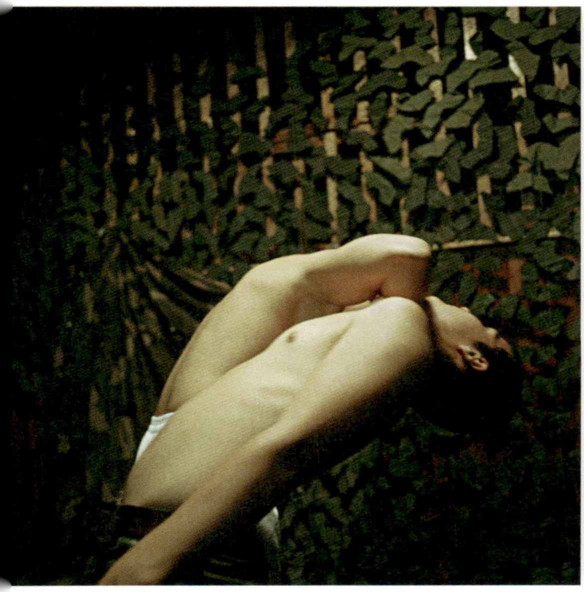
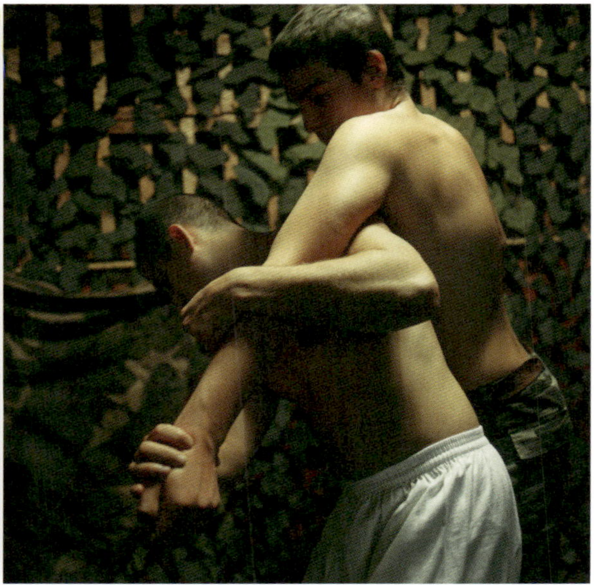
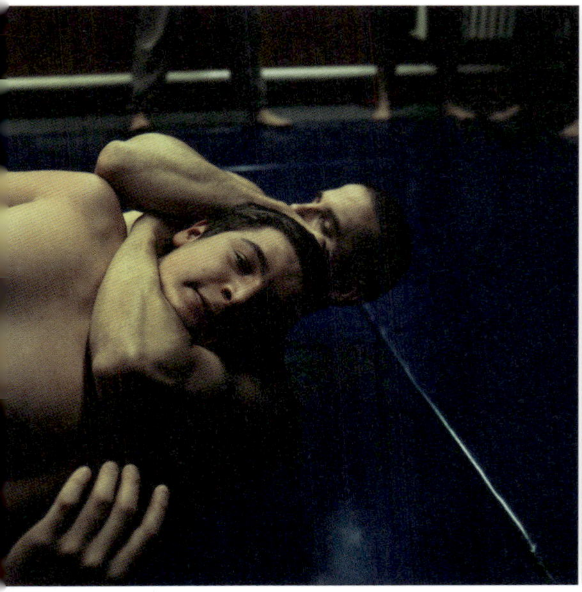
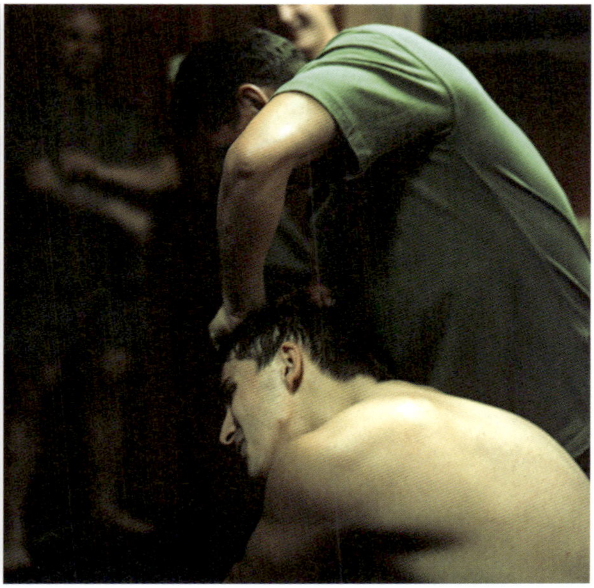

Yet what a filthy dream I woke up to once! I am standing in a room by a desk, behind which is seated an obese, hormonally challenged bonehead, with matted hair, rotting teeth, bags under his eyes, and a sneer on his face: a major, and what he wants is for me to put my signature at the bottom of a piece of paper and accept a post as a prison guard in the central military prison.

So...

I tell him—because what else can I say?—"I'm not suitable." And what do you think the jackass with the overactive glands and the rotten-toothed grin replies? "No one is born to be a prison guard"—that's what he says, by way of encouragement.

Not long after that, I found myself in the prison. I shall never forget my first impression: solid wooden doors lining a cool stone corridor; alongside the walls, widely separated, men standing with hands held behind their backs, foreheads pressed to the wall. They were clothed in wornout military fatigues, without insignia, belt, or indication of rank. Armed guards were standing about at both ends of the corridor. Every now and then, a soldier hurries the length of the corridor; his glinting boots, coloured collarpatches, pistol jiggling on his butt, his supreme indifference, a true provocation. Otherwise, endless time and perpetual, suffocating stillness.

[...], I was scared. As a prison guard, I was terrified of the prisoners. Or rather, I was terrified of coming into contact with prisoners in the capacity of a prison guard. It seemed unavoidable, though, since that was why I had been stuck in the post.

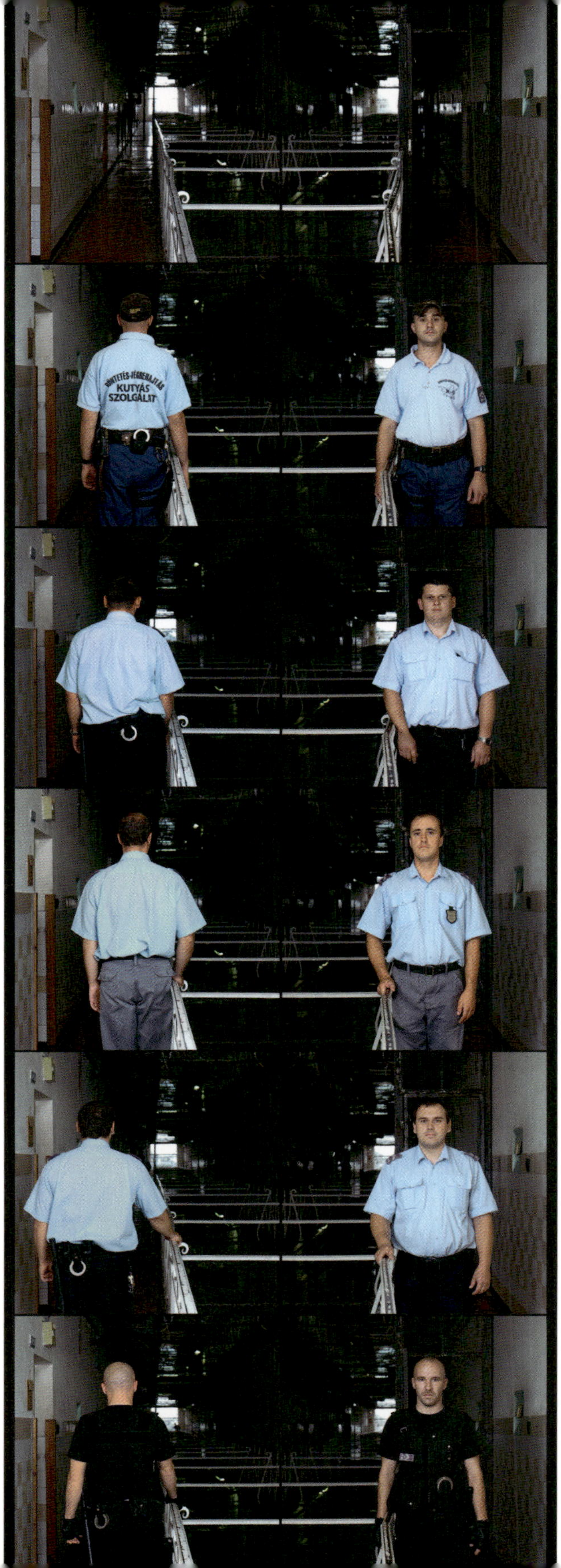
KUTYÁS
SZOLGÁLAT

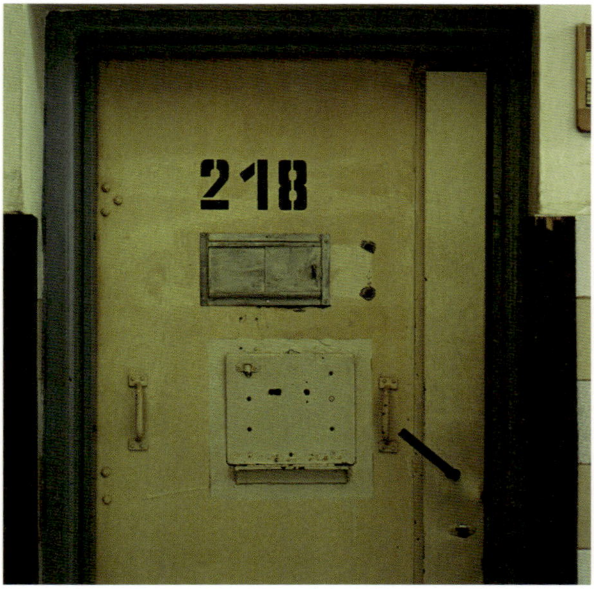
218

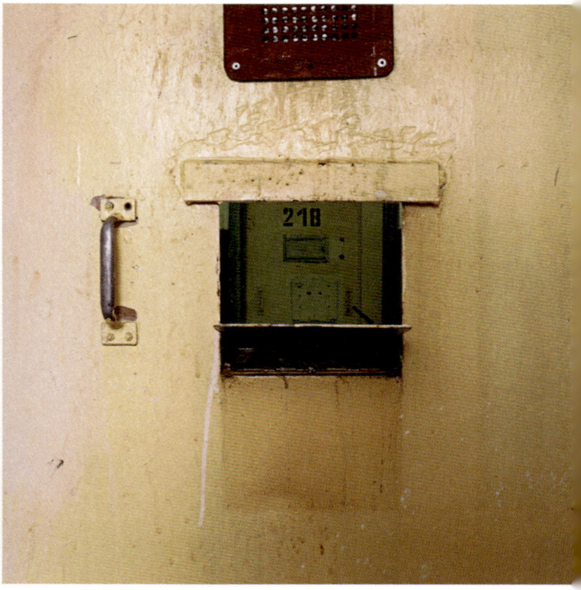
218

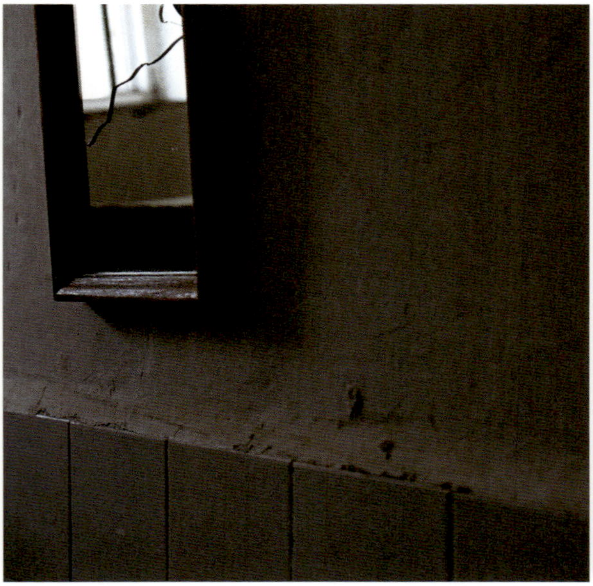

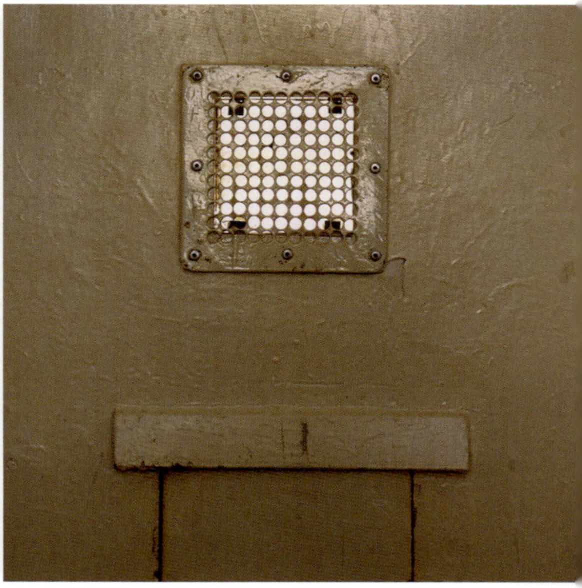

One morning when I went on duty, I was greeted by my fellow guard—a swarthy, stocky, short-legged, and, to all appearences, spruce manikin, except that the prison-guard vocation had taken up residence in him, squatting there like a hideous reptile—with the information that one of the prisoners in solitary confinement was refusing food.

Through the hole I could see a cell: a bunk, a toilet bowl without seat, a washbasin—oh, and of course the man who had to live there. Later on, I tried to look at this as if it were not me looking but a prison guard, but of course it was not long before I had to resign myself to only being able to look as a prison guard, but in particular a prison guard who, sadly, just happened to be me.

I waited until lights out, and when the stillness of the night had descended on the prison—a special kind of tranquillity this is, a lit-up, timeless night, the everlastingness of the nether regions, filled with dull, mysterious, muffled hissing and bubbling underwater murmurs, so to say—I open up the solitary cooler rather like an inflamed wound, with a degree of indistinct hope. "So, tell me why...," I kick off, [...].

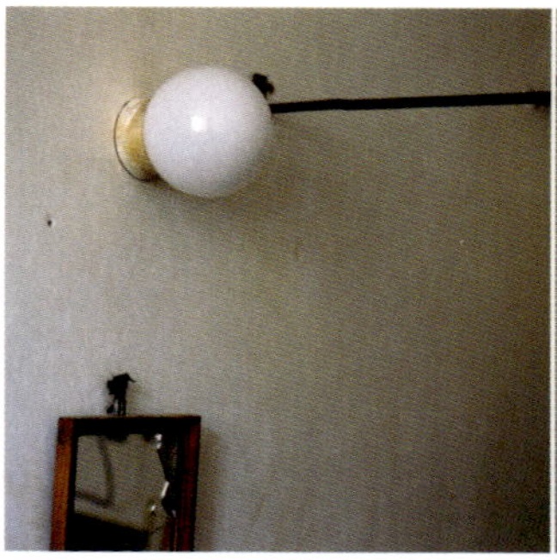
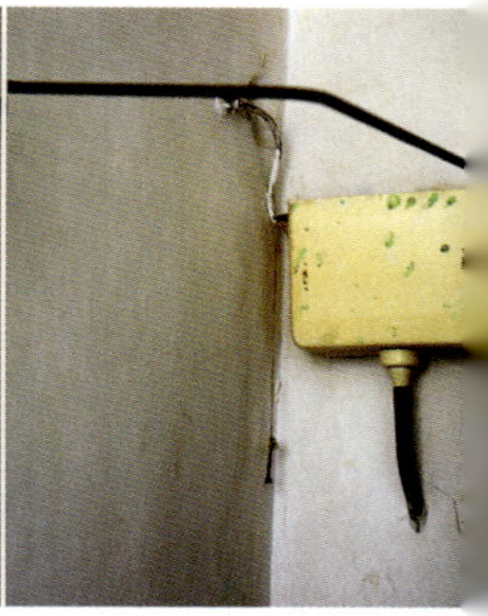
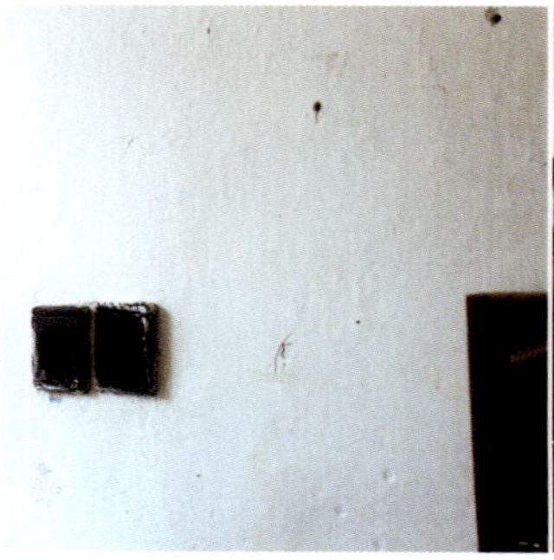
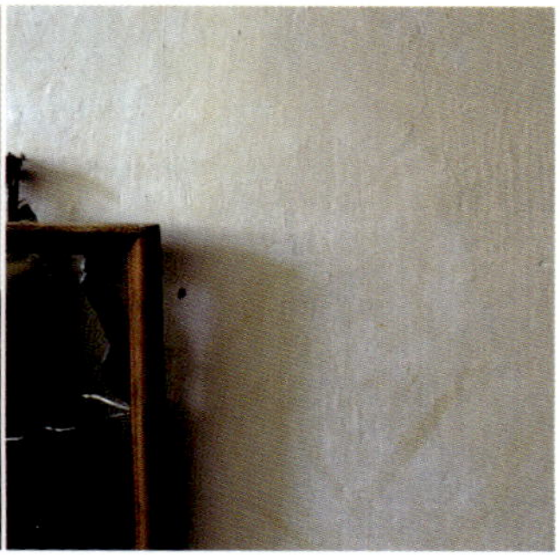
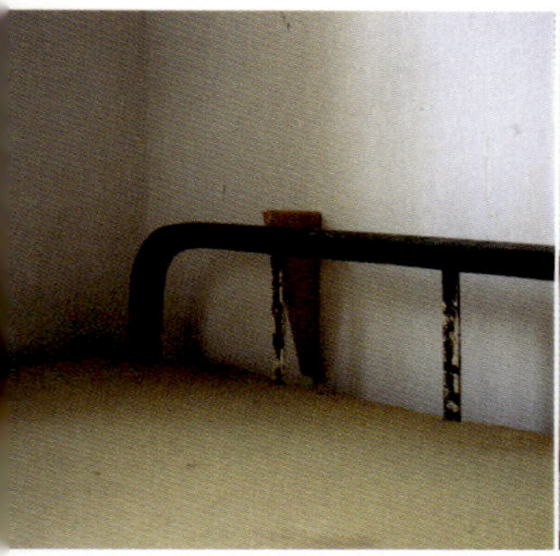
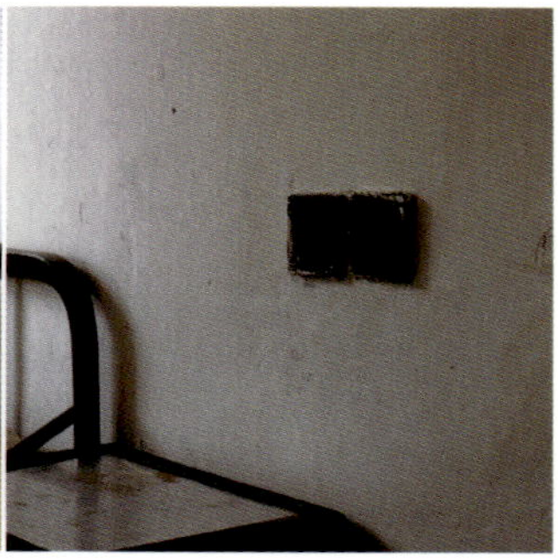

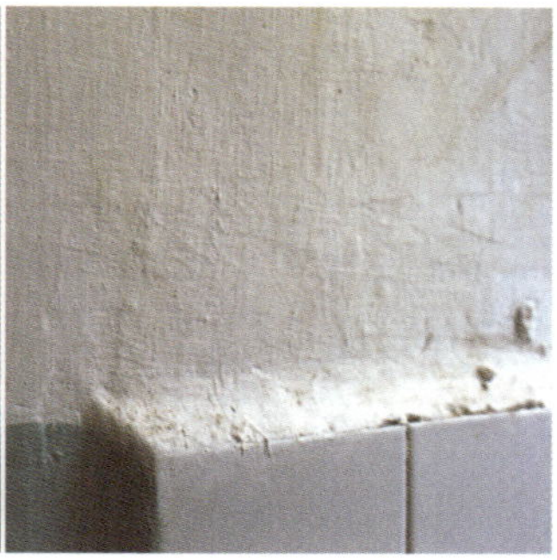

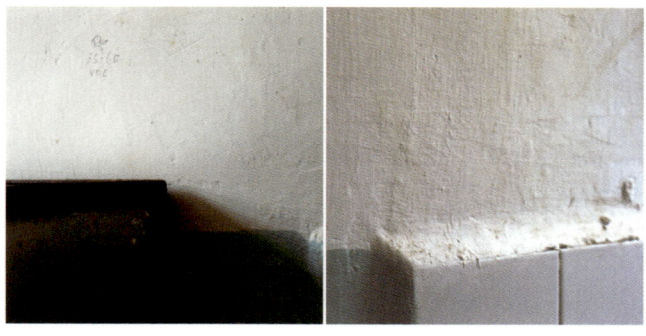

"Do you have the slightest idea what you can expect?" I asked him in the end—and, whatever the rules may say, I had long been addressing him in the familiar form, not out of any contempt, not at all, but driven purely by fraternal irritation, to be precise.

"You're not eating?" I continue. "It's just they won't allow you that luxury here," I laugh, though not out of any amusement. "You can starve, but only if they starve you."

"And don't go thinking that this somehow just happens, as if you were not there or not taking part in it. Or that you can sail through the whole thing without being tarnished by it. You'd be wrong, very wrong!" I exclaim, and perhaps even I am not aware what sorts of fragmentary memories my own words are reopening within me, or what images are welling up from the depths, as from the cellar of a ruined house when the wind whistles through them. "No one who is tortured," I yell, "no one can remain untarnished—that's something I know all too well, and don't ask me how. Afterwards you won't be able to speak of innocence any longer, at best of survival. And if you should have a wish to die, that isn't permitted either. You think they'll feel any pity for you? They'll bring you back from death's door seven times over, don't worry! Dying can only happen in the permitted manner: with them killing you."

That's how I spoke, and my words appeared to be ineffectual.

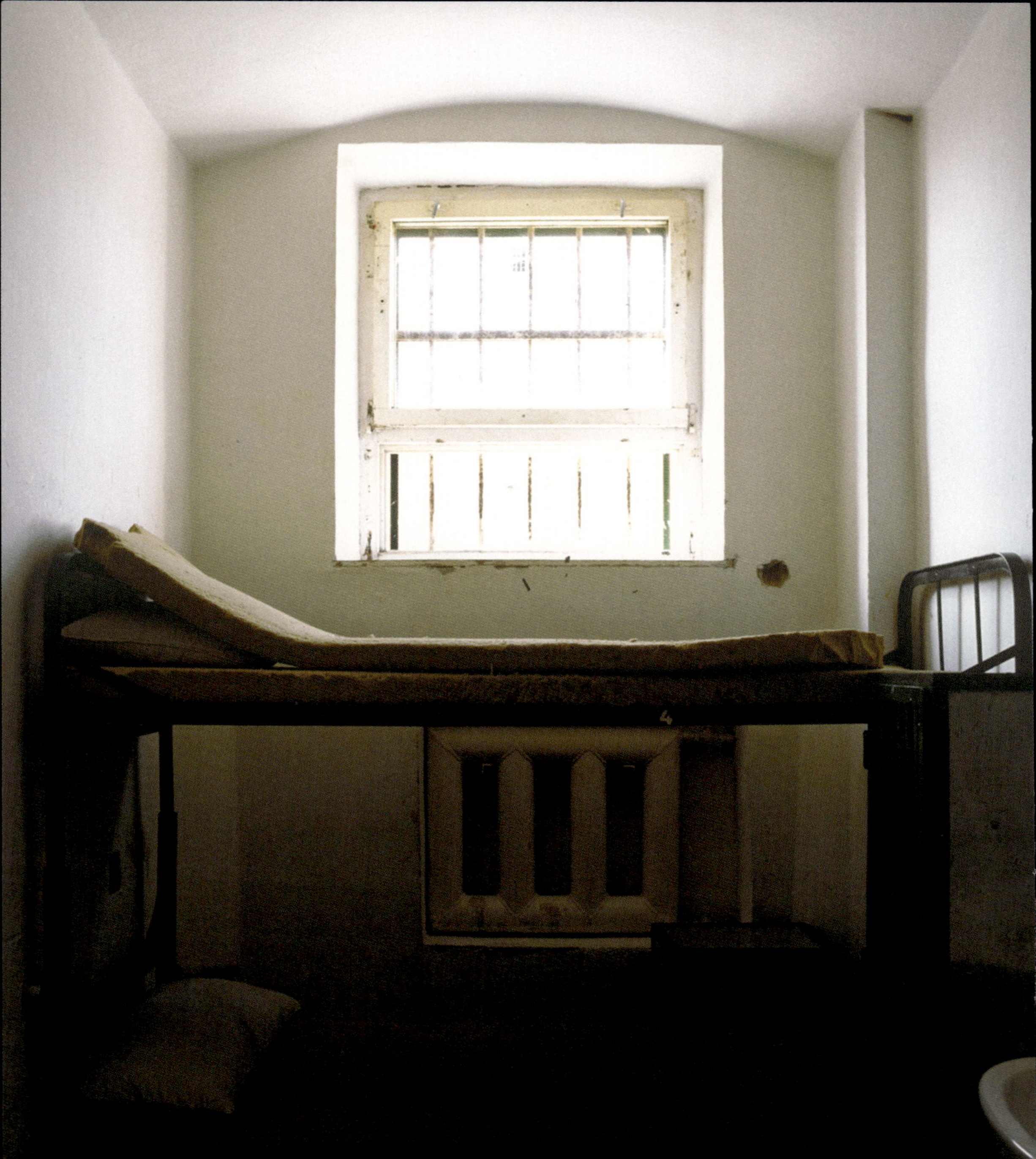

No, all I felt was disgust, sudden despondency, resentment, and again disgust, which included this gaol-breathed prisoner, with whose, for me, all at once so extraneous wretchedness I had been locked together by the moment, through an equally extraneous series of causes, just as it included me. It was all, all, sweeping me toward the simplest solution, of course insofar as I can consider it a solution, to rid myself of that moment, with panic-stricken haste, and in the simplest possible way, as it comes. But I sensed a resistance, [...].

For whatever reason, I took a step forward. A tiny little step only, and I immediately stopped again. Clearly, though, the prisoner may well have misunderstood—or, as I preferred to think at the time: misinterpreted—the movement, because he instantly flinched. But there wasn't much room, and his leg was immediatly caught against the bunk, so he could only lean his upper body farther back, and that was how he faced me. That was when I raised my hand and struck a defenceless prisoner in the face, [...].

Ecce epistola. That, then, is the letter as you may wish it. The "crystal-clear act" (I remember that right, haven't I?), the wound that never heals.
If you wish, by the way, it may even open up the route to the 30,000 corpses.

So, now here I stand (or more specifically, sit) with my story, which I shall hand over to you, not knowing what to do with it. When all is said and done, nothing irremediable happened: no one was killed, and I personally did not become a killer; at most, all links broke down, and something—maybe I do not even know precisely what—has been left lying in ruins.

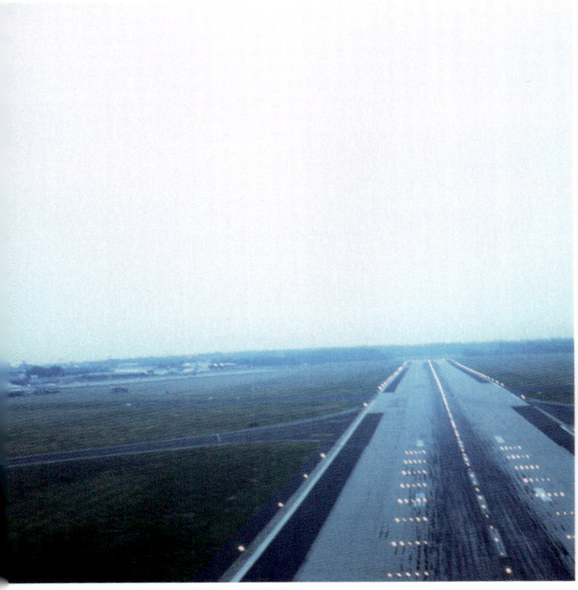
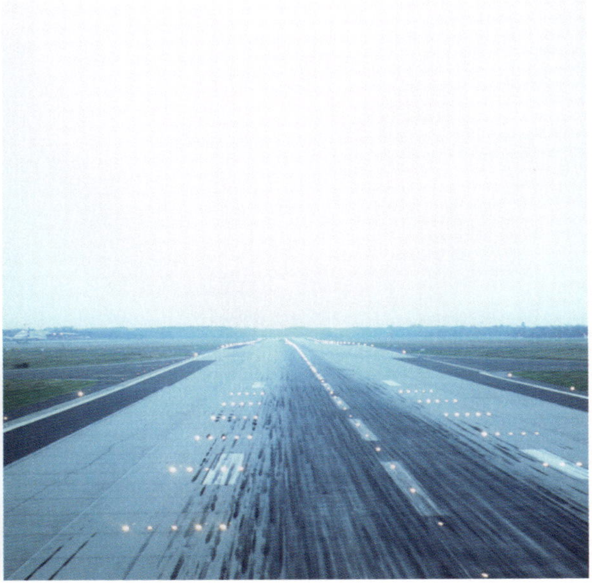
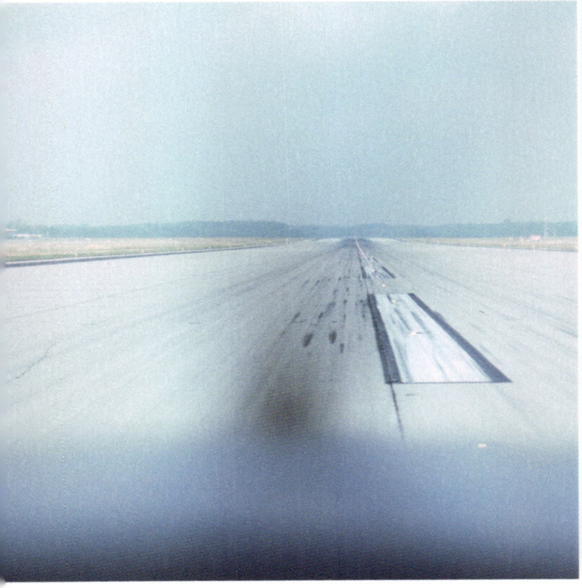
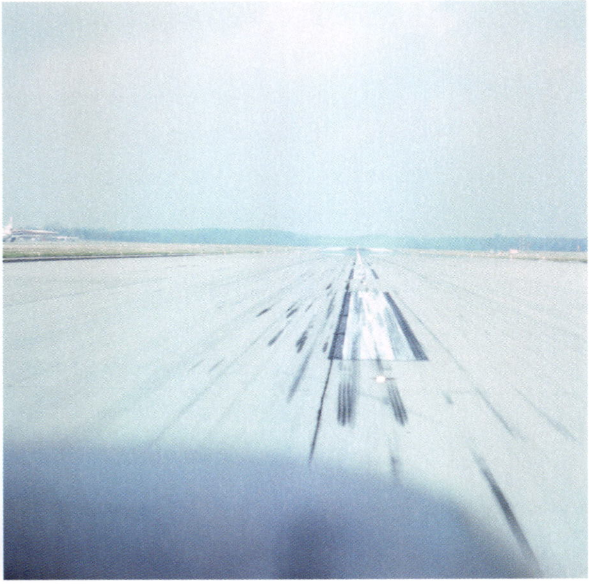

L   [...] Köves could only hope that if he personally was beyond saving, his story could still be saved. How could he have imagined he could hide away, detach himself from the gravity of his life like a stray animal from its chain?

That was how Köves roved the streets, now dawdling, now breaking into a dash, aimlessly and yet, most likely, setting himself an aim as he was going, and of course he noticed that he was sometimes stumbling into obstacles, having to make his way round people, whole groups of people, there being many out on the streets and making quite a racket; he even saw a march, this time a genuine one, with the slogan WE WANT TO LIVE! on the banners raised on high amid the ranks of the marchers [...]. It was probably getting late, though it was still daylight when he turned into the street on which he lived, and he seemed to hear his name being called out among the other cries, though he started only when someone plucked at this arm, it was Sziklai, [...].

"Old chap!" he exclaimed, evidently extremely excited, his hard, olive-tinted face, and the sharp lines etched into it looking like a veritable wood carving, "Get your things together. We'll be coming for you tonight with a truck!"

[...] The fire brigade had been disbanded, the soldiers had gone home, the South Seas had closed, the borders were rumoured not to be guarded by anyone, and a group of people — including Sziklai — who had been waiting long, long years, knowingly or not, for a chance to escape from this city, which denied all hope, this life which belied all hope, had now get together [...].

"Where to?" Köves asked, at a loss to understand, and Sziklai came to an irritated standstill, having meanwhile set off almost at a run, and although he had little idea where he was going Köves more or less mechanically tagged along with him.

"Does it matter?" Sziklai fumed. "Anywhere!…" He set off again. "Abroad," he added, and in Köves's ear the word, at that instant, sounded like a festive peal of bells.

He walked on for a while without a word, head sunk in thought, by Sziklai's side.

"Sorry, but I can't go," he said eventually.

"Why not?" Sziklai again came to a stop, astonishment written all over his face. "Don't you want to be free?" he asked.

"Of course I do," said Köves. "The only trouble is," he broke into a smile, as if by way of an apology, "I have to write a novel."

"A novel?!" Sziklai was dumbstruck. "Now of all times?…You can write it later, somewhere else," he went on. Köves continued smiling awkwardly:

"Yes, but this is the only language I know," he worried.

"You'll learn another one," Sziklai said, waving that aside, almost tapping his feet in impatience: it looked as though other urgent matters were calling him.

"By the time I learn one I'll have forgotten my novel."

"Then you'll write another one." Sziklai's voice by now sounded almost irritated, and it was more for the record than in hope of being understood that Köves pointed out:

"I can only write the one novel it is given me to write."

From 1960 to 1973 Kertész wrote his novel *Sorstalanság* (Fatelessness). After the manuscript was repeatedly rejected, the novel was finally released in 1975 by the *Magvető* publishing house. In *Fiasco*, Kertész reflects on the story of how this first novel came about and its rejection. Both works are part of his fatelessness trilogy.

11

CELEBI

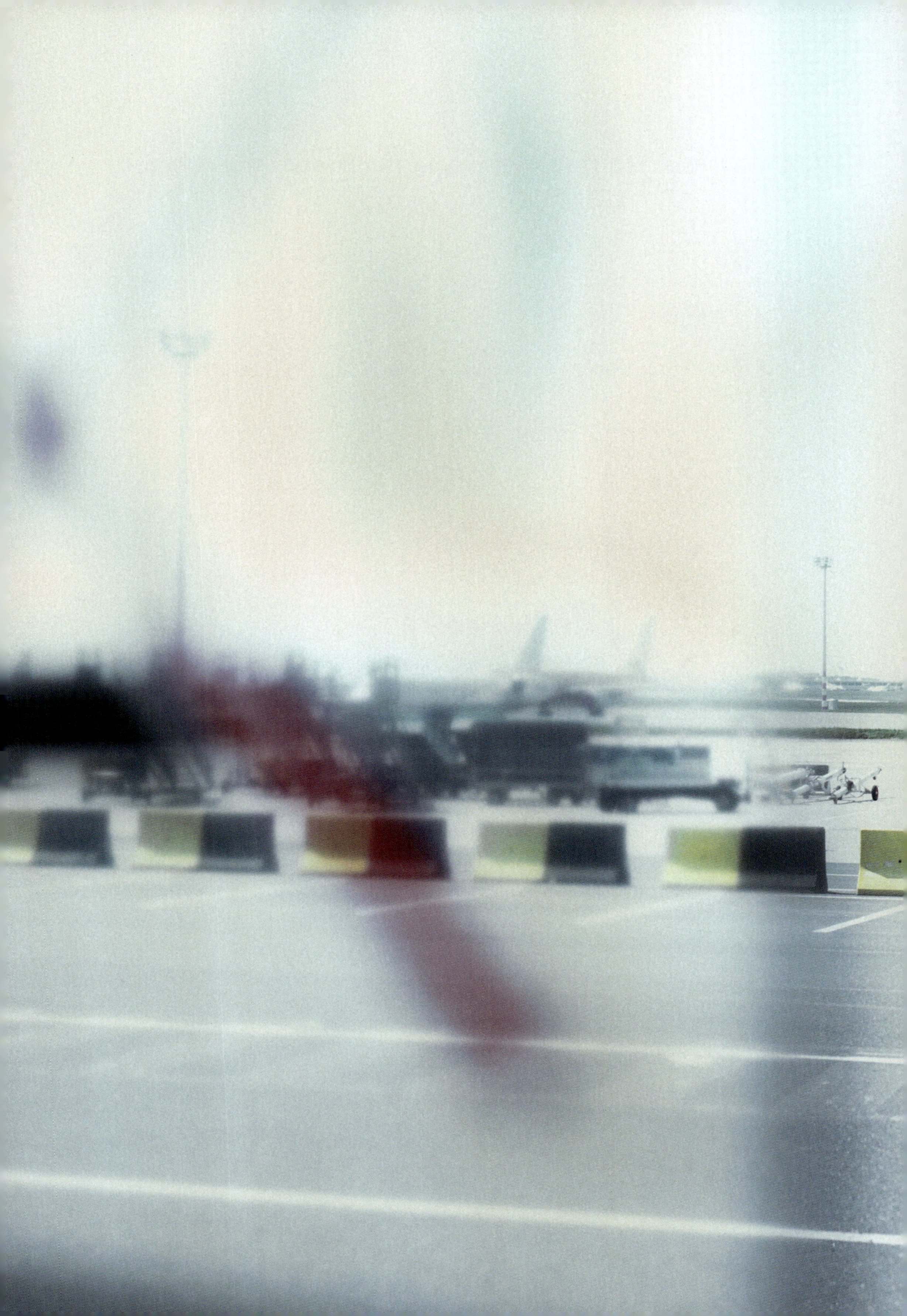

Collapse of reality and the concreteness of the concrete
Epilogue by HINDERK EMRICH

"When I think about a new novel, all I think about yet again is Auschwitz. No matter what I think about, I always think about Auschwitz. Even if it seems like I'm talking about something completely different, I'm talking about Auschwitz. I'm a medium of the ghost of Auschwitz, Auschwitz speaks through me, out of me."
Imre Kertész: *Galley Boat-Log*, 1999

From 1978 to 1988, Imre Kertész spent ten years of "forced labour" working on *Fiasco*, a text consisting of two parts: in a detailed framing structure, Kertész makes the fiasco of the rejection of his book *Fatelessness* as his subject, and describes his many attempts at coping with this, writing his next novel with an almost traumatic precision. The second part contains the actual narrative novel structure and ends with the decision to write *Fatelessness*. Both parts of the novel are related to each other dialectically: on the one hand, the framing of the novel forms brackets for the before and the after; on the other hand, the novel itself has a circular structure.

Fiasco is concerned with something like "conquering life through the novel" and, at the same time, "invalidating life through the novel." It is about the fact that life "over there—somewhere into the night, or even beyond that, [...] [had] hit rock bottom" (p. 125): "It may have begun at birth—or no, rather with his death, or to be more accurate, his rebirth. For Köves had survived his own death; at a certain moment in time when he ought to have died, he did not die, although everything had been made ready for that, it was an organized, socially approved, done deal..." (pp. 125, 126).

And it is about the antipole in the sentence "We want to live!" (p. 357).

An airplane appears above the city with a man who comes from nothingness, and who is also an apparent nobody, a person who steps out of a non-life into a surreal life. One in which it is said that this life is commencing—before he has any identity, any sense of warmth, security or a place of his own—with a notice of dismissal. A life dismissed before its coming into being.

This situation is so monstrous that a framing introductory chapter of 135 pages is devoted to it in which the question is radically posed of the identity of that person who is writing, and who, by writing, creates an identity for himself, who pens a world for himself. This contradictory situation of writing, this "galley-boat work," this "endless loop,"[1] this situation marked at one and the same time by the notion of arbitrariness, of

---

[1] Albert Camus' essay *The Myth of Sisyphus* is of central importance for Kertész' novel *Fiasco*. Kertész escapes death just like Sisyphus who outfoxes it three times. But as punishment, Sisyphus has to roll a rock again and again up a hill, just like the old boy in *Fiasco* who writes further and further on his only possible novel.

writing a novel of some kind or other, yet on the other hand of writing the "only possible novel," I would like to set in relation to a comment by Imre Kertész: "You can't imagine Auschwitz. It's such a degrading, inhuman form of life that you yourself, as someone who has experienced it, are amazed at how you were able to endure it."[2]

The novel *Fiasco* is concerned with the philosophically-psychologically (exciting) subject of "trauma and concreteness." In this way, the question arises of why the background framing story of the novel—one which has been omitted in the photonovel by Riedel, Pratschke and Hámos—of why the minute precision of the concrete depiction of the writing situation assumes such a prominent position in the novel.

It is concerned with the question of memory in a Hegelian sense of "re-membering," of the possibility of creating a medium between the present life and the traumatic past; it is concerned with recollection sketches.

The introductory pages place the processing of memory in a thematic context: of treating one's own melancholy and the impossibility of being traumatized to develop a coherent self-identity. That person is described who, to some extent, proceeds with the written text of the novel, who "makes an object" of the person of the traumatized one. It is the one to whom the self says: "He glued me." As the novel recounts: "I have had enough of my walk; I sit down. I snuggle down, nestle deep into the armchair, adopting a curled-up posture as if in some Brobdingnagian womb. Maybe I am hoping I shall never have to emerge from here, never go out into the world. Why should I?" (p. 77)

In his work *Time and Narrative*, Paul Ricoeur remarks that humans are barely able to develop an absolute "metaphysical" identity for themselves, but create instead a "narrative identity," i.e. a specific mode of self-referentiality through the forms of speech in the narrating of their own life stories.[3] Thus, Kertész' novel is a metaphor for the structure of our coming into being: our life as such is a fiasco. We are failing to the extent that we are always in a backyard of our being, of our existence, but never seem to remain in the being, in the existence, itself. And something is created out of the traumatic experiences of the protagonist (the old boy, Köves), of the author himself in a certain sense, which can be understood per se as a radical metaphor for life: the fiasco of the impenetrability of being. This impenetrability (in a manner similar to that with Franz Kafka) is the center, the heart of this

---

2 Imre Kertész: interview, conducted by Sönke Petersen, published on 31.01.2007, www.bundestag.de/blickpunkt/103_Parlament/0701/0701011.htm
3 Paul Ricoeur: *Time and Narrative*, Vol, 3: Narrative Time. Chicago 1991: The University of Chicago Press

great novel. "Destiny [...] would have bogged me down in the moment, dipped me in failure as in a cauldron of pitch: whether I would be cooked in it or petrified hardly matters.[4] I was not circumspect enough, however. All that happened was that an idea was shattered; that idea—myself as a product of my creative imagination, if I may put it that way—no longer exists, that's all there is to it." (p. 70) When one considers this dichotomy between conceptual language and life, then one could word it as: we live evermore in an "unredeemed situation." We live in the fiasco that our language, our terms and concepts, our thoughts, our senses, our spirit, are not capable of describing us, nor of saving us. The fiasco has to do with the insight of always arriving in the background, in the becoming, in the writeable and the sayable, of standing in one's own "shadow," but never in one's "own being," which might grant the underlying person some security and substance. Doing so, the subject of "writing a novel," which arises repeatedly in the novel by Imre Kertész, is a representation of a coming-to-terms-with-oneself; whereby a becoming-something-else occurs, a "narrative identity" (in the sense of Paul Ricoeur) emerges from the "fatelessness" (in the pivotal novel by Imre Kertész).

This becoming-something-else has very precise qualities that describe par excellence the relationship with the spirit and the world of being human in the modern age.

One antidote for the collapse of reality after the trauma, after the rupturing of stability, is the "precision," the willingness of the victim to confront the concreteness of the concrete. For this reason at the beginning of his novel *Fiasco*, Kertész describes the details of his home, his life and his files of thoughts and ideas so precisely in their inner inconsistencies, with perpetual insertions, bracketing and addenda, with a concreteness that extends through to the world of numbers: "This, then, was his (the old boy's) way of ensuring that he caught sight of the ordinary, grey, standard-sized (HS 5617) box file containing his papers. On the grey file, as a paperweight, so to say, squatted (or swaggered) (or sphered) (depending on the angle from which one looked at it) a likewise grey, albeit a darker grey, stone lump; in other words, a stone lump of irregular shape about which there is nothing reassuring that we might say [...]." (pp. 15, 16) The compulsive writing and ordering (concretizing) leads to a kind of precision that has something redeeming in it that can thus develop a function that provides a grip in

---

4 Kertész has suffered a double trauma in the sense of "out of the frying-pan into the fire": first the nationalist-socialist and then the communist dictatorship. The cauldron of pitch metaphor can also be understood as: in the concentration camp "the old boy" was condemned to cook, before Köves then petrified in the communist steelworks.

the sense of a "presence," a transformation in the here-and-now, the present.[5]

The names in the original Hungarian novel—Köves as Stone, Sziklai as Rock, and Berg as Mountain—stand for the Myth of Sisyphus, of how much Sisyphus rolls a rock up a mountain in his stony life, before it then immediately rolls back down again. These names also have to do with the question of what happens when this torture is brought to an end, when the work on the novel is complete? Does it occur that the "task" is then abandoned? This is what the conclusion of the novel is about. It is concerned with the destruction of the destruction, with the abandonment of the task, with the question of nihilism, using the following words: "What is he supposed to do about that?" (with the rock which has worn down into a small stone, that he, whistling to himself and lost in thought, has been kicking before him in the dust). "Obviously, he bends down to pick it up, thrusts it into his pocket, and takes it home—it's his, after all. In his empty hours (and now there are only empty hours in store), he will undoubtedly take it out from time to time. It would be ridiculous, of course, for him to buckle to rolling it uphill, onto the heights of the peaks, but with his senile, cataract-dimmed eyes he contemplates it as if he were still pondering the weight, the grip. He curls his shaking, numb fingers round it, and no doubt he will be clutching it still in the final, the very last moment, when he slumps down, lifeless, from the seat facing the filing cabinet." (p. 361)

---

5 Cf. Michael Theunissen: *Negative Theologie der Zeit/Negative Theology of Time*, Berlin, 1991: Suhrkamp. H.M. Emrich: *Über die Verwandlung von Zeit in Gegenwart im Film*, Vorlesungen an der Kunsthochschule für Medien Köln, Göttingen/*On the Transformation of Time in the Present in Film*, Lectures at the Academy of Media Arts Cologne, Göttingen, 2010, Cuvillier

FIASCO
*A photonovel by Janet Riedel,
Katja Pratschke and Gusztáv Hámos
With fragments from Imre Kertész' book*

EDITED & RELEASED BY CONCRETE NARRATIVE SOCIETY E.V. ASSOCIATION

WITH THE KIND SUPPORT OF
KULTURMUT—A CROWDFUNDING INITIATIVE FROM THE AVENTIS FOUNDATION, STARTNEXT,
STIFTUNG KULTURWERK FOUNDATION OF THE VG BILD-KUNST COPYRIGHT ASSOCIATION,
GERMAN REPRESENTATIVE FOR CULTURAL AND MEDIA AFFAIRS (BKM), HAMBURG SCHLESWIG-
HOLSTEIN FILM FUNDING BODY (FFHSH), KURATORIUM JUNGER DEUTSCHER FILM FOUNDATION,
FILMSTIFTUNG NRW FOUNDATION, MEDIENBOARD BERLIN-BRANDENBURG FILM BODY.
WARM THANKS TO IMRE KERTÉSZ AS WELL AS TO ALL PERSONS AND INSTITUTIONS FOR THEIR
ASSISTANCE WITH THE PHOTO WORK AND WHICH PARTICIPATED IN THE CROWDFUNDING FINANCING.

1ST EDITION 2014, REVOLVER PUBLISHING

© THE ORIGINAL TEXTS, IMRE KERTÉSZ, "FIASCO" (1988), ORIGINALLY PUBLISHED
IN HUNGARIAN AS "A KUDARC" BY SZÉPIRODALMI KIADÓ PUBLISHERS, BUDAPEST
© THE GERMAN EDITION, ROWOHLT. BERLIN VERLAG GMBH PUBLISHERS, BERLIN (1999)
© THE ENGLISH EDITION, MELVILLE HOUSE PUBLISHING, NEW YORK. FIASCO (2011),
TRANSLATED BY TIM WILKINSON. PUBLISHED BY ARRANGEMENT WITH THE
PUBLISHING HOUSE AND AGENTUR BRAUER.

© THE SHORTENED NOVEL SECTIONS, KATJA PRATSCHKE

© THE PHOTOGRAPHS, JANET RIEDEL

© THE TEXTS, THE AUTHORS

© THE TRANSLATIONS, FINBARR MORRIN

LAYOUT AND DESIGN: JANET RIEDEL, KATJA PRATSCHKE, FRAUKE WIECHMANN
LITHOGRAPHY: ALEXANDER BOHR, KÖNIGSDRUCK
PRINTED ON OMNIBULK BY KÖNIGSDRUCK PRINTERS, BERLIN
AND BOUND BY BRUNO HELM, BERLIN
PRINTED IN THE EU

© 2014 JANET RIEDEL, KATJA PRATSCHKE, GUSZTÁV HÁMOS,
CONCRETE NARRATIVE SOCIETY E.V. ASSOCIATION AND REVOLVER PUBLISHING
ALL RIGHTS RESERVED. ANY COPIES (INCLUDING EXTRACTS) ONLY WITH
THE EXPRESS PRIOR PERMISSION OF THE PUBLISHERS.

REVOLVER PUBLISHING
IMMANUELKIRCHSTRASSE 12, D-10405 BERLIN
T: +49 (0)30 616 092 36, F: +49 (0)30 616 092 38
INFO@REVOLVER-PUBLISHING.COM
WWW.REVOLVER-PULISHING.COM

ISBN 978-3-95763-102-2

26-8-10 Willems Penricke ④

3 m²

2 m | 1 m | 2 m

28 m² / 25 m²

natuurlijk

2.5

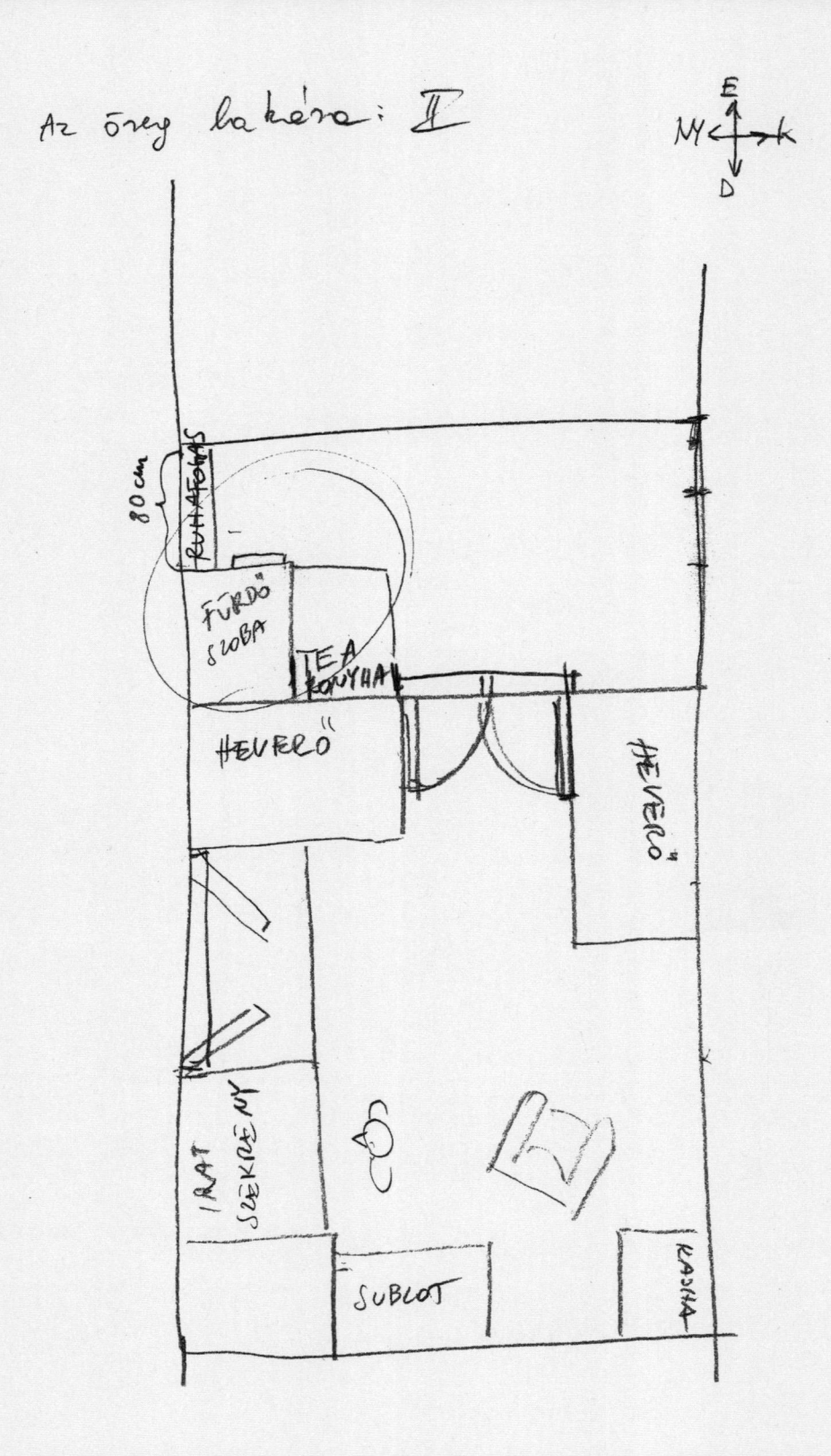

The two drawings by Gusztáv Hámos reconstruct the apartment which Imre Kertész describes in the first 135 pages of his novel *Fiasco*. This is where Kertész's protagonist "the old boy" has written his novel *Fatelessness*.